I0717893

WARNING

This book contains sexually explicit scenes and adult language. It may be considered offensive to some readers. This book is for sale to adults ONLY.

* * * * * * * * * * * * * * * * *

Please store your files wisely where they cannot be accessed by underage readers.

ISBN-13: 978-1988083667
ISBN-10: 1988083664

Other books by Shyla Starr:

<u>Persuasive Billionaire BWWM Romance Series</u>

Stacey is trying to keep a handle on her life the best that she can. She is on the verge of losing her job and her apartment, while taking care of her sick grandmother. Her life takes an unexpected turn when she meets Charlie, who works for the construction company that is attempting to persuade her to move out of her home.

<u>Tenacious Billionaire BWWM Romance Series</u>

Adalia is too proud to accept help from the billionaire playboy, Trent Dawson. How long can she maintain her resolve? The bank is at her heels to repossess her business. To make matters worse, Adalia finds suspicious evidence of Trent's philandering ways. She must determine whether to trust Trent with the fate of her business and her heart.

<u>Elusive Billionaire Romance Series</u>

Billionaire Hendrick is trying to repair his company's image by putting in some volunteer work, building a school and hospital for the impoverished children in Africa. There, he meets a beautiful African American volunteer, Jocelyn. They hit it off right away but does she belong in his world?

<u>Lonely Billionaire Romance Series</u>

Tricia was hired to care for billionaire John's wife, who is dying. An unlikely romance emerges after his wife, Rebecca, gives John permission to pursue his happiness after she is gone.

iii

Ardent Billionaire Romance Series

Deirdre doesn't know what to make of the gorgeous man that seems to be interested in her. His name is Parker Walters and he seems friendly enough. There is just something off about him. Why is he trying the hide the fact that he is the heir to his father's billion dollar software empire?

Fervent Billionaire BWWM Romance Series

Alexandra had never been with a white man before. She had seen William at the café before but she always kept her distance. It was unfortunate that their first chance meeting happened when she dropped her breakfast and spilled coffee all over his expensive business suit.

Get the latest update on new releases from the author at:

https://shylastarr.com/newsletter/

This book contains all the stories of the "Audacious Billionaire BWWM Romance Series"

1 - Love Eluded

Chante is torn between staying close to a man beyond her league, and fleeing from him to spare herself from a hopeless position. But she finds she is propelled into a place where she needs to confront her doubts and cast her fate aside to follow the dictates of her heart. Damned if she does and miserable is she doesn't, how will Chante face the events that will lead her to a place of pure happiness or to the pits of a broken heart?

2 - Love Astray

Chante is slowly getting over her heartbreak from the enigmatic Jared Lowell. Realizing that he is not the right man for her, she is ready to fall in love again and finds happiness once more in the arms of her new lover, Dr. Leo Cadman. That is until Jared's presence at the hospital stirs up all the emotions she used to have for him. Torn between the affections of a man who adores her and a sexual attraction she cannot contradict, who will Chante gamble her heart with?

3 - Love Abided

Chante finds herself accepting a marriage proposal from a man everybody considers 'the perfect man'. She knows she is the luckiest woman on earth. But although she could fool everyone else, she could never fool herself. Her heart belongs to Jared Lowell. It always had since the day she first laid eyes on him. Caught between a farce of an engagement and a growing intimacy between her and Jared, which will win in the battle for the truth... her heart or her mind?

Audacious Billionaire BWWM Romance Series

Books One to Three

By Shyla Starr

Table of Contents

Book One

Chapter One

CHANTE GREEN knew she was going to be late for work…again.

"Shit…," she mumbled, impatiently tapping her foot as she craned her neck to see if the bus was anywhere in sight.

She could almost see the look of annoyance on the face of her supervisor, Nurse Betty Lebowitz. It was the third time this month alone and Chante knew she was hanging by a thread. She could lose her job at New York General Hospital, and she needed that now more than ever.

Chante genuinely hoped that Nurse Betty would be a little sympathetic and cut her some slack. After all, the supervisor was familiar with the reason Chante was under a tremendous amount of pressure. Her brother Markey had ALS or Amyotrophic Lateral Sclerosis, also known as Lou Gehrig's disease.

A catastrophic disease that was initially misdiagnosed, Markey now had only partial control of his legs. Looking back, he was always clumsy as a child, often falling or stumbling, but everyone said it was just a phase and he'll eventually outgrow it. But as the years progressed, Chante noticed the slurred speech. Her mom eventually took him to a specialist who, after rigorous testing declared the boy was in the second stages of ALS.

Things became even more difficult when Chante's dad contracted malaria and eventually died from it. Chante and her mom, both heartbroken over the sudden death, struggled to meet the special needs that were required to deal with ALS. Her mom, having had experience in caring for sick children, took on most of the responsibilities. When swallowing became too hard, they took turns giving him food through a feeding tube. Mom would bathe him; help him use the bathroom; exercise his arms and legs to prevent atrophy, until her son's disease took its toll on her as well.

Driving one night to buy medicine at a nearby pharmacy, she was too preoccupied to notice the red light at a street intersection and was hit on the driver's side by a passing truck. She was in a coma for three days before she succumbed to her injuries. At nineteen years old, Chante was left with an enormous responsibility towards a brother who was not even of her own blood, but who meant more to her than anything in the whole world. He was her only family.

Chante didn't remember much of her early childhood years, except shuttling from one foster home to another. At six years old, she was considered too old by most couples wanting to adopt a baby. The shy and gawky black girl with soulful green eyes was never chosen. Unable to find a good family for her, city officials decided to turn her over to the State Institution for Unwanted Children. On the eve of her departure, a woman came in, noticed her cringing in a corner, and approached her.

Chante believed she was an angel with blond hair falling softly around her shoulder. But it was the sweet voice that calmed her enough to reach for the hand that was offered to her. The woman was enamored with the emaciated child and decided to adopt her. The lady, Hannah Green, brought her home and introduced her to her husband, Caleb, a Mulatto who was delighted to see her. Chante felt an instant kinship with the dark-skinned stranger. Hannah made her feel like the daughter they never had. Both were missionaries who went to far-flung places on medical missions.

Chante spent her growing years travelling to places most children would have found depressing. No electricity, no running water, and sometimes just a hut to sleep on at night, if they were lucky. Otherwise, it had to be in a tent or under the stars. Children with malaria, TB, pneumonia, measles, and countless other maladies constantly filled their days.

From her adoptive parents, Chante learned compassion, dedication, and sympathy for the sick. No one was turned away. There was always room for one more.

Chante blossomed under their care. The lost look in her eyes gradually changed to confidence. She learned her ABC's under Acacia trees with other children. Instead of children's books, medical books were her constant companion. She couldn't read most of the words, but the pictures amazed her. It was no surprise that she declared she would become a doctor someday. She changed her mind after she found her passion working alongside the nurses, who took care of their patients day in and day-out.

It was during one of these missions that her mom and dad discovered that they were expecting a baby. Chante's innate insecurity returned. She knew she was adopted and was afraid to be given away again. Her parents, seeing the troubled look on her face, assured her that she would always be a part of their family. They loved her so much like she was their very own, they said. That restored her confidence so much so that when the baby finally arrived, Chante immediately fell in love with the little bundle of crinkly skin and puffy eyes. No one seeing them for the first time would ever doubt they were brother and sister. They looked so much alike… same curly hair and bronzed chocolaty skin complexion.

When Chante's dad contracted malaria and eventually died from it, they moved to a smaller house. Maintaining the big sprawling colonial house where Chante grew up became too much for her mom. Money was scarce with the little pension she was receiving from her work as a missionary and Chante was in her last year in high school.

They found a modest apartment in Queen's where they had better access to local facilities and clinics for her brother Markey. They joined a local chapter for ALS victims trying to understand and cope with their situation at home.

Chante remembered her childhood passion of becoming a nurse, her caring disposition making her a natural. She looked into the idea of nursing school and found work as a candy striper in a hospital nearby. She enjoyed the experience of helping care for the sick. Her duties revolved around making a patient's stay in the hospital more pleasant. She delivered the patients' meals, helped feed them, occasionally read to them, and assisted in releasing them from the hospital. When the nurses found themselves overburdened, Chante gladly took on more responsibilities.

Everyone who knew Chante was fond of her. Chante Green was an attractive girl with a heart of gold. She cared for her patients and treated them like they were family. Friends who knew her well concluded this was her way of giving back. She had found her purpose and it gave her the experience to deal with her own personal situation at home with Markey.

After six months of volunteer work, she decided to take a course as a Certified Nursing Assistant after her Volunteer Coordinator assured her of a paying job at New York General Hospital. Chante was elated. She signed up for a three month night-course when her mom met the accident that took her life away.

Chante never fully grasped where she got the strength to carry on. Those days were like dark clouds hovering over her head ready to engulf her in an instant. Making the funeral arrangements so soon after her dad's passing, talking to Markey and making him understand that it was just the two of them from now on, and trying to cope with her CNA classes… there were lots of instances when Chante just wanted to give up. She often cried herself to sleep, burying her head in her pillow so Markey wouldn't hear her moaning with grief. The enormity of what lay ahead was just too much for a young girl and she was often just very scared about the future.

Thankfully, the ALS organization came to her rescue. They assisted her in every way they could until

Chante got back the determination to continue. She eventually finished the three months CNA course and landed her current job at New York General Hospital.

"Oh, thank God," Chante whispered in relief as she spotted the silver-gray public transport that would bring her to work with hardly any minute to spare. The bus was less than two blocks away, lumbering slowly beside the sidewalk, picking up riders as they waited. Chante made sure her ID was in her bag, as well as her cell phone. She needed to be able to keep in touch with Liza, the caregiver who was currently with Markey. She was the reason Chante was running late. Liza called in an hour ago and told Chante she was held up at home with an emergency.

Chante panicked, knowing that she couldn't afford to miss work, but Liza thought she was only going to be a half-hour late. If Chante could hold on, she'd be there, she promised. Markey was seated in the living room watching his favorite cartoon. It always broke her heart seeing him with a blanket across his legs. He should be out playing basketball or hanging out with his friends, Chante thought.

"Hey Chant," Markey called out when he spotted her checking in on him, "You off to work now?"

"Soon as Liza comes. She said she'll be a half-hour late today," Chante replied.

"I can manage. It doesn't look like I'll be going anywhere," Markey replied with a naughty grin.

Chante approached her brother and tousled his hair. She knew he hated that. "I know, but I'll feel better knowing that you're with someone," Chante countered.

"You worry too much about me. I'll be fine…," Markey reassured her.

Chante let out a sigh and replied, "I know kid, we both will." As soon as Liza knocked, Chante gave her brother a peck on the cheek and ran out the door.

"C'mon…c'mon…," Chante urged the bus that was still a half a block away. She was so intent on making the bus go faster that she hardly noticed a figure approaching slowly from behind until the man put his arm across her shoulder.

"How's my favorite girl… I haven't seen you in a while," the man said.

Chante gave a surprise shriek at the sudden contact, swiveled around and saw who it was. "Jimmy…," she gasped with relief, thankful it wasn't a mugger. And then as Jimmy's presence dawned on her, a sudden fear crept inside her chest. She had been trying to avoid Jimmy Derollo for weeks now. She didn't answer his calls, hoping he would get the message and stop. He was the last person on Earth that she wanted to see now that she was in a rush to get to work.

"Jimmy…I'm in a real big hurry right now. I can't stay and talk…," Chante said stiffly as she struggled to get away from the arm that was still across her shoulder.

"Hey… hey… hey… aren't you even glad to see me?" Jimmy asked with a nasty sneer.

Chante knew better than to antagonize him. Jimmy Derollo was a shady character that lived in the same neighborhood. He had a Mohawk haircut dyed in purple shade and a nose ring. He wore a black leather jacket with skin tight jeans and leather boots. Before she knew better, Chante thought he was cool. This was the period in Chante's life when she didn't know what to do and where to go. Her mom's death left her confused and terrified. When she met Jimmy, he seemed eager to know more about her and she ended up telling him about her troubles. Jimmy was all ears and a shoulder to cry on. Chante found his attention gratifying and thought she found a rock to hold on to in her very confusing world.

They went out on a few dates until one day she ended up in his apartment. He passed her a joint and assured her it was alright. Chante never smoked pot in all her life. She coughed and sputtered, unable to catch her breath. She really thought she was choking to death until the effect of the drug hit her. From then on, she was like putty in his hands. They had sex right on the couch with Chante a captive participant, unable to resist. She just remembered feeling lifeless with no control over her arms as Jimmy pounded into her repeatedly. She woke up a couple of hours later, naked, on his bed, with Jimmy snoring away next to her.

Chante felt pain all over her body. She had no memory of what had transpired between them. An overwhelming sense of shame swept through her entire being. She didn't need to remember anything at all. Her imagination more than made up for what she didn't know. She saw him a couple times more and each time they were together, Chante realized exactly just how bad a decision she made thinking he was special. Jimmy was not only into drugs. He was also a convicted felon out on parole for extortion. Chante always believed in giving people second chances, but instinctively she knew Jimmy Derollo didn't belong in that category.

Chante looked around helplessly. Jimmy, seeing the confused look on her face, made a move and came even closer. He held a hand out to her chin and raised her head to kiss her. Chante turned her head away at just the right time for his kiss to land on the side of her face. Chante didn't know what possessed her as she let a resounding slap land on his face.

"What the fuck…," Jimmy said as he grimaced in pain. He made a move to grab her by the shoulder as the bus rolled to a stop in front of them. The automatic doors hissed open and a voice hailed out to them.

"Miss…is that man bothering you. I can use my radio and call 911…," the voice of the driver called out loudly.

Jimmy let go of her arm immediately. He was on parole and didn't need this right now.

"It's alright…I'm ok…," Chante replied, knowing that for now at least she was safe from Jimmy. She immediately moved towards the safety of the bus door.

Jimmy gave her a sinister look as he muttered under his breath, "this ain't over yet, bitch… I have something on you that you don't know about."

Chante was still within earshot to hear the threat in his voice, but she didn't stand around to know what was behind it. She had to get to work and away from this disgusting man who, unfortunately, was an ex-boyfriend. She resolved to momentarily forget about Jimmy and focus on the next eight hours of her shift.

Chante reached the back entrance to the hospital and headed straight for the rows of gray metal lockers in the basement, entered the ladies bathroom and donned her uniform. She studied her reflection in the wall mirror, splashed cold water on her face, and removed a tube of toothpaste and brushed her teeth vigorously. Strands of hair entangled around her nape. She took a moment to comb her dark hair back into a severe bun. Reaching for the light switch, she turned it off and opened the door to the hallway leading to the Nurse's Station on the second floor.

Amos, the hospital janitor was removing bleach from the closet when he saw her. "Good Morning, Ms. Chante. You shoo is a sight for tired eyes," Amos greeted her.

"Good morning, Amos. What's the floor like today? Should I hide from Nurse Betty?" Chante replied back gaily.

"Oh, I think she'll hardly notice you're late agin. B'sides, she should give you some slack, coz of that lil' brother of yours and everythin'…," the old man replied.

"I surely hope so, Amos. But I'm at the bottom of the food chain. So…," Chante replied with a grin.

"I did see Nurse Betty few hours ago and she look like them chicken that got its head chop' off and hadn't made the connection," Amos informed her.

Chante laughed out loud. "Why… what's causing the buzz this time?" Chante asked curiously.

The hospital was always on heightened alert. Chante had already accepted that as part of hospital life.

"Oh…I dunno… some bigwig came in a helicopter…set the whole place in a-tizzy. Some rich folk, I reckon…," Amos answered with a shake of his head. He had been working in the hospital a long time that nothing ever ruffled him.

"Well, alright then…," said Chante, waving as she hurried to report to the head supervisor. She sincerely hoped Amos was right and Nurse Betty wouldn't notice she was five minutes late.

"Chante…" A voice hailed her as she turned a corner of the hospital wing. Glancing around, she recognized Debbie, an intern recently assigned to her wing.

"Hi Debbie," greeted Chante.

"Have you heard…?" Debbie asked. She knew everything happening within the many walls of NYGH. She made it her business.

"Heard what… I just arrived for work. I expect to get another lecture from Nurse Betty about the ethics of coming in early. I'm late again, you know," Chante explained, hoping that Debbie would take the hint and let her go. Debbie wrinkled her nose. She knew what that was like. Suddenly she remembered why she was so excited and the sparkle returned to her eyes.

"Guess who was just brought in early this morning. You'll never guess in a hundred years…," Debbie challenged.

Chante knew Debbie was raring to tell. So she shrugged her shoulders and said, "Who?"

"Mrs. Samantha Lowell. The mother of *the* Jared Lowell," Debbie answered with a girlish shriek.

The name didn't register and Chante's face showed it. "Who is Jared Lowell," a clueless Chante asked. She was certain that Debbie would give her the rundown even if she wasn't that interested to know. A patient was a patient regardless of status. That much she learned from her adoptive parents.

"Duh… just the richest man alive, the most sought after bachelor in the whole America," Debbie replied, hardly believing that Chante didn't recognize the name.

"You've never heard of him?" she asked in disbelief.

"Nope… sorry… Forbes Magazine is not a guilty pleasure," Chante replied with a laugh. She imagined a balding man with a beer belly, smoking a cigar and dressed in fancy $500 suits. "What's the mother here for?" Chante was curious to know.

"Ohhh…according to the grapevine, Mrs. Lowell suffered from chest pains late last night. Their family physician suggested that she be brought to the hospital. But apparently Mrs. Lowell refused, saying she was just tired. The doctor thought otherwise and called her son, Jared Lowell, who was in Geneva and flew in by private jet to be by his mom's side. She was airlifted here via their private helicopter," Debbie narrated, her eyes glowing with excitement.

"Oh, Chante, but he is absolutely gorgeous… ohhh… I hope I get assigned to watch over his mom…," said Debbie, drooling.

"Good luck then…" Chante waved her off, forgetting in an instant everything she heard from her. And then Debbie added, "Nurse Betty is losing her mind. The General Director has been on her case since the chopper landed. Seems like they're undermanned right now, what with four other nurses being on sick leave and all…"

Chante realized that the sooner she announced her arrival, the higher the chances that Nurse Betty would let her tardiness today slip by. She was right.

"Oh Chante… I'm so glad you're here. I need you to fill out these forms. I just don't have the time for that right now," Nurse Betty said as she handed Chante a huge stack of papers.

"Alright," Chante replied as she heaved a sigh of relief.

"And don't think I haven't noticed that you're late again," Nurse Betty said with a disapproving look on her face. "You should be so lucky I need all hands on deck today."

"Of course, Nurse Betty," Chante replied with chagrin. She should have known that the supervisor had always one eye on the clock.

Chapter Two

Chante spent the next couple of hours filing documents and transporting medical records to the appropriate hospital departments. She checked on the insurance liabilities of the patients on record and made sure everything was up-to-date. It was mostly clerical work that she used to do as a candy striper. She didn't mind though because she wanted to be useful while she was on duty.

Occasionally, Nurse Betty would hand her a couple of lab specimens and requests for drugs from the pharmacy. Before she knew it, her eight hour shift was over and she had a crick in the back of her neck from all the paperwork she did.

She stretched out her tired body and was about to head for the exit when Nurse Betty came running down the hallway.

"Listen, honey… I know you just came out of an 8-hour shift, but do you mind doing another 3 hours more? We're seriously understaffed right now," Nurse Betty explained.

Chante was eager to leave and see Markey before he went to bed. But Nurse Betty had a pleading look on her face. Chante realized that this was an occasion to get on her good side.

"Alright, Nurse Betty… let me call home and check on Markey… see if Liza can ask someone to replace her. I'll join you in a while," Chante replied with a smile. Nurse Betty smiled in relief. She knew Chante never declined a request. She always came through.

Nurse Betty was busy checking on patients' charts, updating reports, and giving out assigned posts when Chante walked back in.

"Chante, I'm glad you're here," she said, while pulling a chart from the bottom of the pile. She lowered her voice and ushered her away from the other nurses hovering around the station.

"I've assigned you to Suite 247," Nurse Betty informed her. Chante was surprised. Suite 247 was reserved mostly for celebrities, government officials, dignitaries, and other prominent people; it was a hotly contested commodity among the nurses. She glanced at the name on the chart and read 'LOWELL, SAMANTHA' written in big bold letters. The name sounded familiar. And then she realized this was the person Debbie was talking about early this morning. Well… it was the son she was drooling about mostly.

Nurse Betty saw the surprised look on her face and said, "Well… are you going to start slobbering like all the other idiot nurses? Goddammit… you'd think these bitches have never seen a handsome face before. Nurse Ruth dropped a bedpan… that new girl Debbie mistook a benzo for a vitamin pill… giggling and tittering like a bunch of hormonal school girls. I'm surprised Mr. Lowell hasn't called Director Whittle yet."

Nurse Betty sighed in exasperation and said, "Please, Chante… I've had a full day trying to make do with these foolish nurses and their raging hormones. I just need a reading… pulse, temp, etc… you know the drill."

"Yes… of course, I can manage that," Chante reassured the supervisor. Chante's rubber-soled shoes shuffled soundlessly towards the room where a 'STRICTLY NO VISITORS ALLOWED' sign hung. She opened the door and entered.

The suite was huge compared to the other rooms in the hospital. Curtains were drawn tightly over glass windows. Darkness was dispelled by the warm light of a bedside lamp. A custom made retractable black and silver bed that looked like it belonged in a five star hotel, was pushed into the rear wall between the closed windows. Tucked neatly with a quilt up to her a waist was a woman silently reading a book. She held up a forefinger to her lips indicating that Chante should be quiet.

From the glow of the reading lamp beside her, Chante saw that the woman had silver-gray hair that fell to her shoulder. Her regal bearing was complemented by grayish-blue eyes under perfectly arched brows, a small patrician nose, and thinning lips.

"Mrs. Lowell, I'm Chante. I didn't mean to disturb you. I just need to make some readings and then I'll be out of here again," Chante explained softly.

"It's all right my dear, I needed some company anyway. We just need to be quiet. My son is asleep. The poor boy had been up the last 24 hours worrying about me," Mrs. Lowell explained.

Chante nodded as she glanced at a smaller bed a few feet away. This must be Jared Lowell, the man who had set the hospital nurses on fire. Chante did not see anything except a hulking figure. That side of the room was in semi-darkness.

She took the old woman's temperature and pulse reading and said, "Everything looks normal. Can I do anything for you before I go?"

"Well…I really need to… pee," Mrs. Lowell answered.

Chante recognized the look of embarrassment on her face. Somebody with her pedigree probably felt awkward asking assistance for such a personal need. She entered the bathroom and saw a bedpan and carried it towards the bed.

"Uhmm… what's that?" the old woman asked, with what sounded like horror in her voice.

"It's a bedpan," Chante replied, feeling foolish.

Of course it was a bedpan.

"I know it's a bedpan. But why are you bringing it to me?" Mrs. Lowell asked.

"You said you wanted to pee," Chante replied with some confusion.

"I'm not peeing on any bedpan," the old lady declared, as she struggled to get out of bed.

Chante nearly dropped the bedpan as she jumped across the room to stop her.

"You can't get out of bed…," she said as she tried to push her back.

"I can if I want to pee… and I'm not peeing on a tin can…," the old lady answered obstinately.

"Alright, I'll help you…. but please take it easy. You can have a dizzy spell after being in bed," Chante replied as she took hold of the old woman's arm.

"What the fuck do you think you're doing?" a voice called out from the other side.

Chante was taken aback and looked in the direction where the voice came from. As the figure rose and emerged from darkness, Chante barely suppressed a gasp. And as he approached nearer, Chante caught her breath. If she didn't exhale soon she'd turn blue in the face.

The man was stunning. Brownish-blond hair over a chiseled face, thick brows over cobalt-blue eyes, a finely sculpted nose, high cheekbones, and a good strong jaw line. A slight flaw of a cleft chin only managed to enhance the Adonis effect.

The buttons on the rumpled shirt was open all the way, revealing a smooth hairless chest. Portions of a six-pack lay visible against the narrow opening. He was barefoot and Chante thought that she had never seen more perfectly formed toes in all her life.

The upper part of his pants hung low over a narrow waist and Chante had to exert all her strength of mind and body not to stare at the swelling that was etched against the crotch of his pants.

"*Oh my God!!!*" Chante's heart skipped a beat as she clamped her mouth shut.

If this man managed to wake up each time with that erection, he should be considered a lethal weapon. Now she understood what the brouhaha was all about.

"I-We…," was all she managed to say.

"Oh, don't get your panties in a bunch, Jared. Chante was just helping me get to the bathroom," Mrs. Lowell admonished her son.

You're not supposed to be out of bed…," Jared replied, giving Chante an annoyed look like it was her fault.

"I can if I want to go to the bathroom," his mom answered, glaring up at him.

Chante was caught between mother and son locked in a battle of will.

"Oh…alright," he conceded as he came near to take his mom's arm.

"Chante can manage…Can't you, dear?" the old lady asked as she pushed her son away.

Chante managed to nod her head mutely. Samantha Lowell's remark about the panties in a bunch somehow managed to steady her equilibrium. She tried to dismiss the image from her mind and the laughter that was slowly forcing its way up her throat.

But the problem with trying to overcome one's laughter in an absurd situation is that the more it persists on being set free.

Chante felt her body heave as she let out a slight titter hoping to release the funny sensation inside her head.

"I'm sorry…," she managed to whisper to the old woman as she guided her towards the toilet.

"It's quite alright, my dear, sometimes he needs to be put in his place," replied Mrs. Lowell, tapping her arm slightly.

Chante kept her back to Jared Lowell as his mom entered the cubicle. It wouldn't do to let him see the amusement on her face.

"Well…don't just stand there like a statue. It usually takes her a while to finish her absolution," Jared remarked from behind.

Absolution…really? Couldn't he just say pee? Chante kept a straight face.

She squared her shoulders, determined to stay where she was. She had a job to do and if it meant staying by the door till Mrs. Lowell finished with her absolution, so be it.

After a few seconds more, Jared added, "You look like an ass standing there by the door."

"At least my panties are not in a bunch…," Chante remarked, before she actually realized she said that out loud.

A stunned silence followed. Then she actually heard the man snicker before she got the courage to slowly turn around and face him.

"You are a feisty one, aren't you?" Jared remarked, standing just a few feet away from where she stood at her post.

Chante found his proximity stimulating and unsettling at the same time.

"Look Mr. Lowell…," Chante began.

"Jared…," he cut in.

"Jared…err… Mr. Lowell, I'm here on orders to look after…," Chante continued.

"I know…I know…," said Jared, cutting in once more.

Then he did a totally unexpected thing. He moved even closer until they were just inches away from one another.

"You understand my concern, don't you?" he asked, with an earnest look on his face.

Chante didn't realize that she could go beyond unsettled. *This*… was unsettling on the verge of panic. She felt like a deer caught between the headlights of on an oncoming car. Well… her eyes were just as startled as she tried to lower her lids to prevent them from blinding him as well.

And it didn't help any that he reached out a finger to her chin and raised her face to meet his.

Chante never understood the overwhelming desire that washed over her. Instinctively, she opened her lips as if waiting to be kissed. Jared's arm snaked its way behind her ass, copped a feel, before pulling her even closer.

Chante could at this time feel the hard authenticity of the bulge that earlier was just a figment of her imagination.

She closed her eyes as if in dream waiting for the kiss that was about to come. Then through her fogged brain, she heard the water flushing from inside the toilet, which brought her back to reality. Her eyes flew open in a snap.

"Gotcha…," Jared mocked as he released her.

Chante was stunned, shocked, and then mortified.

This man just played her. And she fell hook, line, and sinker.

Just then, the door to the suite opened and Nurse Betty entered with the Hospital Director, Jonathan Whittle, behind her.

He announced that he was there to accompany Mrs. Lowell to have her MRI done.

"Is that really necessary?" Samantha Lowell protested.

"It's just part of a series of tests that I want you to undergo. We must rule out all possibilities of a heart condition," Director Lowell answered in a condescending voice.

The four of them, the Director, Nurse Betty, Mrs. Lowell and her son, discussed briefly as Chante stayed rooted to the spot.

"Oh, alright…," said the old woman. "But please let Chante stay. I will need her after the procedure. This isn't going to take too long, is it?" She asked Nurse Betty impatiently.

Nurse Betty shook her head in response to the question. Chante took it to mean that she was not allowed to stay, so she headed awkwardly for the door.

"Stay!" The director barked at her.

A wheelchair was brought in to ferry Mrs. Lowell to the third floor and Chante hurriedly positioned herself behind it, ready to push the old woman out of the room.

"I said stay!" the director reiterated.

Chante was starting to feel like a dog having difficulty understanding her master's command.

She meekly let go of the chair and moved out of the way as the procession headed out the door. Unfortunately, it didn't include the son who had a wicked grin on his face.

If she could make herself disappear, she would, but she didn't dare leave the room until the old woman returned.

She set about tidying up the bed trying her best to ignore the presence of Jared Lowell.

"You really don't have to do that," he proclaimed as he plopped onto the pillow she was trying to smooth out.

Chante jumped back, startled. Her sense of dignity was being trampled and he was really starting to annoy her.

"Humph…," Chante retorted allowing her irritation to show. She didn't care. He was being obnoxious and she wanted him to know it.

Thankfully, no one was around to witness her momentary faux pas. Chante struggled to retrieve her professional demeanor, reached for the patient's chart and made a pretense of studying it. She didn't even notice he had gotten out of the bed and was standing next to her now.

Close…much too close, her brain informed her.

Too close not to notice how his brows crunched together like he was in deep thought, tense, or possibly irritated over something.

"What?" Chante asked, unable to control her rudeness.

If he insisted on taxing her, she would show him she wasn't taking any more of it.

About what happened earlier, I'm sorry, that was uncalled for," Jared apologized.

Chante was surprised by the unexpected apology. But she wasn't quite ready to give in yet.

"Oh, you mean groping my butt while your mom was peeing? I totally understand. I assume that's what you rich guys do," Chante replied in a voice dripping with sarcasm.

Jared sighed. Chante thought he looked really ashamed, but she wasn't sure. Guys like him were beyond her league.

"Tell me what I can do to make up for it…anything," Jared said earnestly.

Chante thought about it. If he was genuine, which she sincerely doubted, it was payback time.

"Kiss me then…so I can tell all the other nurses who have the hots for you what a lousy kisser you are," Chante replied.

She really just meant it as a joke. But looking back, she wondered where she got the sagacity to challenge him that way.

"Why you little imp…," Jared declared.

With one fast move, Chante found herself in his arms. His hands crossed around her waist, pulling her close. One hand reached up and grasped her chin firmly. Chante watched with a mixture of horror and fascination as his lips slowly descended down on hers. His breath wafted between parted lips.

Her initial reaction was to struggle, tell him she was just kidding, but the eyes that gazed deeply into hers had a hypnotic appeal. Chante felt her protest vanish as her knees turned to jelly. Her hands grasped the side of his hips to keep from falling.

His lips were warm and soft against hers, a gentle kiss meant to impart a message that he was a good kisser. But Chante was surprised by her own reaction as she opened her mouth slightly and bit him gently on the lower lip.

She heard the intake of breath at her audacity. Jared's tongue entered her mouth in a French kiss as his hands crept up to her breast and fondled them against the fabric of her uniform. Chante felt the world tilt around her feet. Her arms reached up, clasped the back of his neck to bring him even closer.

She felt his hand travel inside her blouse caressing her waist before travelling upward under her bra until she felt the warmth of his palm against her bare breast. His fingers searched her nipple and as he grasped it between his thumb and forefinger, Chante knew she was lost. The pleasure shot all the way to her groin.

"Jared…," she whispered huskily, recognizing the desire blooming between her thighs.

"Shhh…," Jared replied.

"Your mom…," Chante protested.

They won't be back yet…," Jared whispered before giving her a torrid kiss once more.

"We can't…not on the bed…," Chante protested horrified at the thought.

"I know…," Jared replied between her parted lips.

He reached down and hoisted her legs so that she straddled him upright. Then, without breaking a sweat, Jared carried her into the bathroom.

Once inside, he thrust her against the porcelain side of the wash basin as his mouth came down hard on hers once again. With the wall against her back and his entire body molded against hers, Chante felt his erection through the thin fabric of her dress. She wiggled her hips slightly, allowing her crotch to feel him.

His hands frantically searched for the zipper on her back, unzipped it, as Chante allowed the upper garment to fall against her lap. Her bra hung askew against her navel.

Jared's lips traveled down her neck and towards her ear. Chante could feel his ragged breathing as he lowered his mouth and gently sucked on her nipple. His hand groped her other breast as he rolled his palm and squeezed her.

Chante's arms wound their way around his neck in a frenzy. Every pore in her body screamed to be taken by this man. She could feel the rippling muscles on his chest as her hands feverishly tried to open his pants. She fondled him and felt the rocklike hardness of his penis as it reared free from its confines.

Chante knew they didn't have much time. The clandestine act was its own feverish thrill.

She pulled her pants down together with her thong panties and let them settle against her ankles. When Jared reached down beneath her, the touch of his fingers on her clit sent her body into a delicious spasm. He began to rub her…slowly, repeatedly and with controlled precise movement. She couldn't believe the heat that engulfed her. The hair on her skin stood on ends. She was on fire.

Jared stretched out his arms and used the wall to support him as Chante clung to his neck. With her hand around his penis, she positioned it against her notch, thrusting her pelvis towards him, feeling the rigid cock as it slowly entered her vagina.

Slowly at first, and then increasing his rhythm bit by bit, Jared explored and filled her entirely. Holding her down so he could feel her deep inside, Jared grunted like a beast in heat. Chante felt her orgasm explode inside, as with one last powerful thrust, Jared followed. He buried his face into her neck, back arched, body twitching with the remnants of his lust.

As their breathing subsided, Chante was struck with the enormity of what just happened. She never intended for things to come this far. She pushed him aside and pulled up her pants, struggling awkwardly to adjust her bra and fumbling with the zip on her blouse.

She had to get out of here. She had to put some distance between them. She hardly met his eyes as she opened the bathroom door, ignoring his voice calling out her name as she fled the room.

To hell with Director Whittle. She could make up an excuse for Nurse Betty why she disappeared. What she wanted right now was to crawl into a hole.

Damn Jared Lowell… The thought lingered for a few extra seconds as she ran into the night like the devil was in pursuit.

Chapter Three

Chante stared at her reflection in the bathroom mirror. Seven hours of sleep had restored her equilibrium. There was an undeniable sparkle in the emerald green eyes. She had a secret, one that she wouldn't ever have the guts to share with anyone. No one should ever know what transpired in a bathroom of a patient in NY General Hospital. And who would even believe her?

She felt like she won the lottery. Heck, this wasn't something she could add to her achievements in her resume. Still, the memory brought a smile to her face that she tried to hide from her brother, Markey.

"Why d'you look so happy?' Markey eyed her suspiciously.

Do I…? she responded nonchalantly.

"Maybe because I have called in sick and will be with you the next three days?" she answered and was gratified with a loud "whoopee."

She had decided on taking the spineless way out. She had no intentions of seeing Jared Lowell once again after what happened.

Whenever her conscience attacked her, she comforted herself with the thought, "We were two consenting adults, so it's fine…"

She hoped that when she returned to work, mother and son would have been gone.

"… transfer to some fancy health facility or wherever billionaires go to recover," Chante grumbled under her breath.

The idea made her feel despondent as her stomach plummeted.

"So what if I never see him again?" she asked herself.

But she did spend a lot of time on Google and was surprised at the stack of information there was about him.

"… Jared Lowell touted as one of America's most eligible bachelors…"

"…Scion of Jared Lowell, Sr. and Chairman of Lowell Enterprises that span three continents…"

"… Receiving his diploma from Harvard Business School…"

There were photos of him as a young boy atop a Shetland pony with sweeping long shots of mountain ranges behind him, and a more recent one with his arm slung carelessly across the shoulder of a stunning brunette.

Chante searched for information about the girl, but found none. Instead, she felt a stab of pain pierce her heart.

"So… he has a girlfriend…what did you expect? A guy like him probably has a girlfriend behind every door he opens, including bathroom doors," she grumbled under her breath.

She donned her scrubs hurriedly on the fourth day not wanting to be late again. She subdued the blooming optimism of seeing him again. Life would be so much simpler if both were gone by now.

The hospital entrance was swarming with paparazzi. Chante's heart skipped a beat. Unless a movie star or another celebrity was confined, this could only mean one thing. Jared Lowell was still in the building.

The funk she carried the last three days suddenly disappeared.

"At least I'll still get to see him… even from afar," she consoled herself.

Chante was willing to accept scraps at the moment.

She made her way hurriedly to the station on the second floor. Nurse Betty was handing out time patient charts to the other nurses. They all looked eagerly at the charts. Chante saw how each face fell with disappointment.

"I was hoping to get room 247…," one said.

Dream on bitch… I'm getting that today…," declared another.

I'll take a 24 hour shift, Nurse Betty, if you give me 247 now…," enthused another.

There was a lot of good-natured teasing among the ladies. Chante was doubtful Nurse Betty would give it to her after hasty retreat three days ago.

"Now… now… ladies, control your hormones. I do not need a cat fight right now. All of you… *go!*" Nurse Betty remarked sternly.

As the other nurses dispersed, Nurse Betty handed Chante a chart. And to her amazement, 247 were written clearly on the front.

"247 again…?" Chante remarked.

It was difficult to control the sudden wild hammering in her heart. She tried to appear nonchalant, but the sparkle in her eyes didn't fool the Head Nurse.

"I never play favorites, you know that... I wanted you nurse bitches to draw lots… Heck, I would have pulled hair and gouge an eye to get a chance to be near that stud in 247, but there was nothing I could do. He asked for you, Chante," Nurse Betty said.

"He asked for me?" Chante echoed.

Her knees turned to jelly.

"Samantha Lowell is a VIP patient. Her son Jared happens to be the biggest donor to the Hospital Trust Fund. So you can understand Director Jonathan Whittle will give him a witch-doctor or a shaman if he asks for it," the head nurse explained.

It was not easy to control her trembling body as Chante walked the floor towards room 247. With a soft knock, she turned the doorknob and entered softly.

She hardly recognized the room from three days ago. It has transformed into a virtual office. Three telephone lines stood on a console table that was brought in. Two technicians were installing a satellite dish by the window as another crew put the finishing touches on a wide-screen TV mounted on the wall.

Jared Lowell sat upright on a table with a powered-up Mac before him. He was talking into a dicta-phone. He stopped momentarily when he saw her enter. A hint of a smile lit up his face.

"You're late…," he said.

Chante wanted to contradict him as she glanced at her wrist watch. It showed the time at 9:09. Her shift started at 9:00a.m.

"We're sorry for all of these," Mrs. Lowell said, waving her hand over the entire room. "This was the only way he could get any work done while I'm in the hospital…," she explained.

Chante approached her, asked how she was feeling, took her temperature and pulse reading, and administered her medication. She was still a nurse, albeit a befuddled one.

The old woman's cell phone rang and Chante moved away to give her some privacy.

As Mrs. Lowell retrieved her phone, Chante took the time to study her chart. Jared casually sauntered to where she stood. His presence was electric, hard to ignore, especially since her heart was racing.

"Are you planning on staying forever," she muttered under her breath indicating the room which now looked more like an office.

She meant it as a casual comment but came out like a snide remark.

"Would you like me to go…?" Jared asked, with a hurt expression in his eyes.

'No… no… no… sorry, I just meant…," Chante stuttered.

She realized she had no explanation and like the coward she was, she fled the room…again.

Chapter Four

For the next few hours Chante switched charts with some of the nurses who couldn't believe their luck. She needed to stay away from him. Chante wanted to salvage whatever dignity she had. He always managed to make her feel like a bumbling idiot. She was no match for him, she accepted that. She hoped Nurse Betty wouldn't notice.

Just then a commotion ensued at the Nurse's station. One of the girls Chante persuaded to take over just returned crying.

"What's wrong?" Chante asked.

"He's having a temper tantrum… refused to let me take the patient's pulse and temperature… almost threw me out of the room…," the girl sobbed.

Chante was aghast. She imagined what that was like. The guy was obviously a billionaire spoiled brat. But she wasn't ready to go in there yet. She got the chart and passed it on to another nurse, hoping she'd accept it. The girl didn't want it either, tossing the chart back to her like it were biohazard.

Oh…alright…I'll do it," she grumbled as four sets of eyes looked at her retreating back with concern.

Chante knocked and entered with some hesitation.

"Oh, Chante, thank God…," Mrs. Lowell cried, waving her in. Her son was by her side with a contrite expression.

"Mr. Lowell…," she began.

"Jared…," he cut in.

"Mr. Lowell, why…," she tried again.

"Jared…," he repeated.

Chante sighed.

"Jared then… why are you being difficult?" she asked him.

"It was the only way I knew to make you come back," he replied, with a smug look.

Mrs. Lowell gave an exasperated sigh and remarked, "My dear, can you please bring my son somewhere else. Get some air. As much as I adore him, he is getting into my nerves."

Oh Jesus. This wasn't in her job description.

"Ok…," she answered meekly.

It was obvious that the confinement was wearing them both down.

"Are you sure you'll be alright, mom. We'll just get a bite to eat," Jared asked.

"Go…go…go…," Mrs. Lowell answered.

Chante felt her heart soar, but refused to think more of it. This was a request from a VIP patient. How could she say no? But she knew exactly where she could take him. Breath of fresh air? Check.

Outside the hall, she walked ahead of him. If he wanted to come he would surely follow. Jared pulled her back and slipped his fingers between hers.

"Jared, please…," Chante protested, pulling away from him.

But he pulled back again and kept his fingers entwined with hers.

"Jared, please…" She was almost begging.

The touch of his hand on hers was setting her body on fire.

"If I promise to behave, you won't run away again?" he asked.

Chante accepted the truce. Deep inside anxiety bloomed. The flirtation was exciting. But it would not lead to anything. Not with someone like him.

Chante steered clear of the Nurses' Station where the elevators were situated. She didn't want to start another hullabaloo with the nurses. She pushed towards the freight elevator located at the end of the hall.

The elevator took them to the top floor of NYC General Hospital. Few people were about as Chante pressed on toward a set of metal doors at the rear. She twisted the handle and pushed outward.

Dusk had descended on New York City as Chante led Jared towards the railing of the roof deck. A few stars struggled to make their presence felt. Buildings dotted Manhattan like a shroud spread out below. The sky was a dazzling shade of lavender and crimson against an orange sun descending slowly in the horizon.

A comfortable silence ensued. No words necessary to describe the magnificent splendor unfolding before them.

The electricity between them was harder to explain.

Chante wondered how many times he had seen this postcard setting with a girl beside him. She'd seen it often enough whenever she wanted to escape the drama of the hospital floor. Surprisingly for her, today it felt like the first time because he was by her side.

Why did he affect her the way he did? Was it the casual sex they shared? He must be an expert in the game of seduction. She wasn't. She tried to stay away and he didn't like that. Was she expected to play along? She didn't know the answer.

Chante pushed the complicated thoughts aside as Jared stirred beside her.

"Thank you, Chante Green, CNA…," he muttered softly.

The naughty look was back in his face. She watched him turn slowly towards her like a movie reel in her mind.

Chante stepped into his embrace. His arms snaked their way around her waist and pulled her near. She savored the intimacy and closed her eyes. It felt amazing. Their bodies were a perfect fit.

When Jared's lips descended on her, Chante thought
the sky lit up with fireworks like the Fourth of July. In
that single moment, she was willing to take any
chances.

"I like you, Chante…a lot. There's something
different about you," Jared said, his chin resting softly
on the top of her head.

Chante smiled secretly. That was a good start.

"I'd like to see you more…," Jared continued.

Chante thought she was dreaming.

And then he added, "I was wondering…you
know…I want to set you up somewhere, a condo maybe
…I want you to stop working at the hospital so I can see
you anytime I'm free from all the work I have to do…I
can buy you stuff…girls like that, right? You're free to
do anything you want when I'm not around. See your
friends, watch movies, go to the theater, but I want you
to be with me exclusively, just me…no hanky-panky
when I'm not around."

Chante froze.

"You want me to be your mistress?" she asked with
a shocked look on her face.

"I don't do the boyfriend-girlfriend thing…," Jared
replied hesitantly.

He couldn't understand the look of horror on her
face.

Chante felt like she had just been doused with ice water. Did he even know what he was saying? Everything he said was "I want…I want…," with no regard for what she wanted. Didn't do the boyfriend-girlfriend thing? What was she to be in his life? A sex toy? And once he got tired of her… what then? Would he casually drop her just like his casual invitation to be his kept woman?

Chante stepped back and drew away from him. The look on her face was undeniable, like he just insulted her beyond belief.

"What? What did I do wrong?" Jared asked perplexed.

He really thought she would be ecstatic with his proposition. She seemed to like him a lot. She gave all the right signals. This was the first time a girl reacted the way she did. Mostly, they were only too happy to accept that kind of arrangement.

Chante could hardly speak.

"I'm not that kind of girl," Chante whispered through stiff lips, "I'm not a whore that you picked up on the street."

"Have I ever treated you like one?" Jared asked.

"You just did…," Chante whispered back.

Despite her promise she would not run away again, Chante fled.

The happiness she felt over their kiss had turned into lead that weighed a tonne inside her. She was right the first time. There was no future in that direction. He was offering her a temporary haven that would eventually find her out in the cold once the curiosity dwindled.

She couldn't accept that. Not now that she was confronted with the truth. She was in love with him. His proposition made that realization so much harder to admit. For her sake, she had to forget him.

Forget he didn't see her for who she really was… forget that he thought his money could buy him the affection that she wanted to give him freely, not in exchange for "stuff" he mentioned.

She had to break free. Break the barriers she inadvertently built around her heart when she first laid eyes on Jared Lowell.

Without saying another word, Chante turned around, leaving Jared open-mouthed and wide eyed. As she left the rooftop, she closed the door behind her.

-To be continued in Book 2-

Book Two

Chapter One

"**ARE WE** doing spring cleaning?" Markey Green asked his sister Chante as he eyed the clothes strewn all over her bedroom floor.

"What? No…no…no…" Chante replied, as she pulled another hanger from inside her clothes drawer.

"I just need to find the right one…" she added as she positioned the dress in front of her and stared at her reflection in the mirror.

She shook her head in disapproval. "Too revealing," she muttered under her breathe.

Markey advanced slowly into his sister's bedroom. He didn't want his wheelchair to run into the dresses that were piled haphazardly on the floor.

"Must be a hot date then," he smiled with amusement as his sister began to attack the shelves where her shoes rested.

Chante stopped momentarily. She was surprised at her brother's spontaneous perception. She smiled trying to mask the concern in her eyes. He had grown so much thinner these last few months. His ALS had progressed so much faster than she thought.

"And what do you know about having a hot date, hmmm…" she said as she tousled his hair.

"Well…enough to notice that you're excited once again. These last few months you just seemed… sad." Markey replied.

Chante felt a twinge of guilt. She honestly didn't realize her brother noticed at all.

"Was I that bad…" she asked as she sat down on the bed.

"Bad? Nah, you were just sad." Markey answered wryly.

"Yeah, I guess I was…but I'm ok now…so don't you worry about me kid." Chante replied.

She never told him about the way she felt. In fact she hasn't told anyone about it. Who would believe her anyway? It isn't everyday that a good-looking and wealthy... very wealthy... Jared Lowell asked you to be his sex toy.

Chante tried to forget everything that happened that day on the roof deck of NY General Hospital. She remembered him calling her name as she pushed the metal doors aside and ran towards the freight elevator. She punched the button on the lift and went all the way to the basement where she knew she would be safe. She was confused, her mind was in a whirl, and she wanted to stay away from prying eyes. She stopped by a wall and there amidst rows of empty cars she slumped down on the hard cement floor as despair and disillusionment brought waves of tears that shook her to the core.

"How dare he…" she muttered disconsolately, "he must think I'm scum."

Jared Lowell, heir to the fortunes of Lowell Enterprises had just offered to keep her as a mistress in exchange for a condo and for "stuff" as he called it, even having the impudence to conclude "that's what girls like…"

But Chante didn't have the heart to put all the censure on the scoundrel. She was partly to blame too, remembering what happened between them in the bathroom of the suite where his mother was a patient.

"Shit…" she whispered between her tears.

But it was too late now for regrets. It happened and she had to live with it. In hindsight, she was confused why she even allowed it to come about. Had the patient, Samantha Lowell, or Nurse Betty, and Director Whittle come back and caught them in the illicit act, she would have lost her job as Certified Nursing Assistant, that's for sure.

It was with uncertainty that she reported for work the very next day. She had vowed the night before that she would refuse adamantly, beg even, not to be assigned to Suite 247 once again. But the floor seemed unusually quiet that morning. She learned that Samantha Lowell was discharged the night before. The private helicopter that brought her in brought her out, as well.

"Oh, thank God," was Chante's initial reaction.

She didn't have to suffer the awkwardness of seeing Jared again. Admittedly, she liked Mrs. Lowell. She felt a certain degree of kinship with the older woman. It made her a little sad, thinking she didn't get a chance to say goodbye.

But as the initial relief swept through her body, she was also assailed with a deep sense of melancholy. She won't be seeing Jared Lowell anymore. That, at least, was its own blessing, Chante thought.

The weeks that followed their departure, Chante often had to struggle with her feelings. She tried to focus on her work but often found herself looking out into space. She felt miserable, disconnected, and it took all her effort to keep going about her duty. The world lay heavily on her shoulders.

Nurse Betty took her aside and asked what was bothering her. Chante couldn't look her in the eye. The woman was very perceptive.

"Is this about a man?" Nurse Betty inquired.

Chante nodded her head. The supervisor didn't have to know who. So Chante decided on a half-lie.

"Yes…but it's over now…" Chante answered.

"That's good. If it didn't last too long, then he must be the wrong guy for you. Get out of that hole you crawled into. Someone better should come along for you." The supervisor consoled her.

Chante nodded her head in agreement. Nurse Betty didn't know how close to the truth she was. Jared

Lowell was definitely the wrong guy for her. It's about time she moved on and forgot all about him.

Things were slowly getting back to normal.

One day, Chante was assigned to the Emergency Room. One of the nurses on duty was down with the flu. The ER head called on Nurse Betty if she had anyone to spare for an 8-hour shift.

Nurse Betty was hesitant to send Chante. She didn't have enough experience with trauma. But the ER head assured her that it was only to help out with minor tasks- cleaning wounds, putting on bandages, administering anesthetics. The other RNs and doctors could take care of the rest.

Chante entered a frenzied ER. It was chaotic. The waiting room was filled with people- mothers and fathers, a sister or brother, or someone's cousin- all waiting for a doctor to tell them about the condition of a patient that was brought in.

The six beds were filled. One patient was having an intubation procedure done; another bed had an old man with a nurse having difficulty locating a vein for IV placement. The old man was agitated and kept pulling his arm away. Another doctor was accompanying a patient out for transport by medical helicopter.

Chante immediately got to work gathering bandages, towels, and cotton balls when the door burst open. A distraught woman had a child in her arms. Chante rushed over. The child was convulsing and his eyes rolled towards the top of his head. There was no bed available to put him in.

Chante noticed a trolley earlier just outside the ER entrance. She ran quickly and pushed it towards the woman and her child. A doctor, who was busy sewing up a knife victim, hurriedly took note of the child's condition. The child convulsed once again.

"Nurse… nurse… ", the doctor shouted at Chante. "Get Dr. Leonard Cadman… tell him it's a possible status epilepticus. He's at the doctor's lounge sleeping. GO!"

"Doctor's lounge…doctor's lounge…it must be somewhere near," Chante mumbled under her breath as she ran out of the ER and into the hallway.

She turned a corner and saw the sign on a door and hoped this was the right one. She opened it hurriedly. The room was dark and Chante had to adjust her eyes before she saw a figure huddled on a bed farthest from the door. She approached slowly not wanting to wake up the wrong doctor.

The man was sleeping on his right side and facing the wall. Chante couldn't tell by his name plate that was hidden beneath his crossed arms, if this was THE Doctor Cadman she was asked to call immediately.

Not wanting to spare another second, Chante called out, "Dr. Cadman…"

No response. The man was in deep sleep. But she did notice that this guy was olive-skinned with a crown of cornrows that framed a chiseled face. Thick long lashes fanned out on cheeks that were crunched by the pillow that was under his head.

Chante knew she had to rouse him sooner than later, so she touched a leg that was sprawled on the bed.

"Dr. Cadman…" Chante called out louder this time.

The figure on the bed stirred, opened his eyes, and looked towards her.

Chante had the image of charcoal grey eyes the color of clouds on a stormy day.

"I'm sorry…but if you are Dr. Leonard Cadman, there is a possible status epilepticus in the ER." Chante mouthed the words.

With one swift move, Dr. Cadman was out of bed and on his feet. He searched for his stethoscope that was lying by the floor where he must have dropped it.

Chante saw this doctor was medium built, taller than she was by a few inches, and was a bundle of energy now that he was awake.

"Sex…" he said.

"What?" Chante replied, before she realized he was asking about the patient's gender.

"Boy…about six years old." Chante answered back hoping he didn't notice her initial confusion.

She followed him out the door as he scurried to the ER.

There were no regular nurses available to assist Dr. Cadman so Chante thought she would stay nearby in case he needed assistance.

"How long ago was his last seizure?" the doctor barked at the hysterical mother. She stared back at him as if he had spoken gibberish.

"How long…?" Dr. Cadman repeated.

"Less than 5 minutes ago," Chante made a wild guess, realizing the mother was absolute no help in this scenario.

"Nurse…I need 5cc of…" the doctor said just as Chante rushed to the medicine cabinet.

She knew exactly what he needed- a prefilled syringe with the medication. She was thankful for all the times her mom allowed her inside the medical tent when they were doing medical mission work.

She handed him the syringe, grasped the boy by the neck tilting his head upwards, and opened his mouth to allow the doctor access inside the opening.

"Thanks…" Dr. Cadman said seeing her clearly for the first time.

The effect of the medicine was instantaneous. After 2 minutes the boy's body visibly relaxed and his breathing though still ragged, was slowly getting back to normal.

The little boy reached out and the doctor clasped the small hand with his.

Chante saw the concern and compassion for the little boy who was scared and confused over what just happened.

"It's alright, you'll be alright…your momma is here…" the doctor cooed softly to the boy.

The hysterical mother had calmed down sufficiently to hug her son while repeatedly saying, "thank you…thank you…"

"Nurse…" Dr. Cadman addressed her.

"Err…I'm not actually a registered nurse," Chante explained, "I was sent here to assist. I'm just a CNA."

"What the…" Dr. Cadman replied with surprise.

He didn't have enough time to finish his sentence as the door to the ER banged open once again with a bloody patient on a trolley.

"White, male, approx 26 years old, stab wound on the lower abdomen…" announced the EMT.

It was total chaos for Chante. Emergency cases after another just kept on coming. She lost track of Dr. Cadman as Chante was asked to bandage a patient, administer IV on another, ran to the pharmacy, and comfort distraught relatives.

A few hours later she found herself working side by side with the doctor again. Chante noticed how efficient he was at what he did, often stopping to give a word of comfort to the patient or to a family member. He kept on addressing Chante as "Nurse" giving her instructions what to do after every procedure. Chante followed orders. She could just correct the misimpression at a later time.

Hours flew by very swiftly before a palpable calm finally settled on the otherwise frenetic atmosphere. Chante realized most of the doctors she saw were new arrivals. She thought now was a good time to go. She just needed to inform the ER head nurse she was calling it a night.

"You did very well today considering…" a familiar voice spoke out behind her.

Chante turned around and saw Dr. Cadman had changed from his scrubs to a pair of faded jeans and a white t-shirt. He held a leather jacket in another hand. If Chante didn't know better, she would have mistaken him for a rock star or a member of a band.

"Uhhm…thanks, Dr. Cadman, " Chante answered, as an overwhelming shyness overcame her.

She wondered why the simple remark made her feel good.

"Leo…the name is Leo, Miss…Green," he added after eyeing her nameplate.

"Chante, please call me Chante…" she replied. "And as I said earlier, I'm not an RN."

"I admit you did take me by surprise when you mentioned that earlier. So tell me, Ms. NOT RN Chante. How come you knew what I needed back then with the child?" Leo asked with a twinkle in his eye.

"My adoptive parents were medical missionaries. I grew up seeing convulsive children almost every day. It just came back to me. That's how come I knew," Chante explained.

Leo's grey eyes travelled up and down her face, taking in the exhausted emerald eyes and said, "I see that you are on your way out. Maybe you'd like to have coffee. To tell you the truth I don't remember when my last meal was. I've been on a sixteen-hour shift."

"I really should be on my way…" Chante hesitated.

She couldn't understand why the simple invitation somehow managed to take away some of the fatigue she felt.

"Please…" Leo begged, "I hate eating alone and I promise to drop you off."

"Well…alright then…I'll just get my stuff and meet you in the parking lot," Chante replied as a kind of thrill bloomed in the pit of her stomach.

She immediately changed into her street clothes regretting the fact she didn't bring something nicer to wear. But how could she have known that an attractive-looking doctor would be asking her out to dinner tonight?

She pulled back the rubber band that was holding her hair in a severe bun and allowed the tresses to fall softly onto her shoulder. Clutching her ID, she swiped her time card against the machine and was soon on her way out the back door.

Leo was waiting by a silver-gray Lexus Hybrid, slouched against the hood with his left foot bent back against the grill of the car.

"God…he is sexy…" Chante concluded.

One couldn't describe Dr. Leo Cadman a stud, but his physique showed he did hit the gym. The lean arms were devoid of any adornment except for a silver wrist watch. The V-necked t-shirt that replaced the scrubs from earlier displayed a compact chest that was wide against a narrow waist. The butt was solid and round, sloping down towards firm thighs and sockless feet shod in brown Brooks Walkers.

He immediately straightened once he noticed Chante approaching. He ushered her towards the passenger side of the Lexus and opened the door for her.

"Gallant…" Chante whispered in her head as Leo reached across and strapped her in, his hands brushing softly against the front of her dress.

Chante followed his movements with her eyes as he moved towards the front of the car and onto the driver side before he opened the door and slid in.

"Do you have anywhere in mind…to get a bite to eat, I mean?" He asked in a low mellow voice.

"Please…you decide," Chante suggested. "After all, you're the one who is hungry."

"Great…" Leo replied as he turned the engine and slowly maneuvered out of the parking lot.

Chante found herself mesmerized by the hands that grasped the steering wheel. She had to admit that Dr. Leo Cadman had the longest set of fingers she had ever seen in a man. He could have been a pianist. And she appreciated how efficient those fingers had been as he took care of his patients earlier at the ER.

He popped a disc into the CD player and Norah Jones singing "Come Rain or Come Shine" filled the inside of the car.

Chante relaxed back into the seat feeling the weariness slowly evaporate from her tired body. Instinctively, she knew that there was no need for small talk just now. She really didn't know how she knew, but she felt absolutely at ease in the presence of the doctor she just met a few hours ago?

"The exact opposite of how Jared Lowell made me feel," the thought came unbidden to her mind.

Chante realized she was thinking of him again. She sighed deeply unaware that she made a sound.

"Are you alright, Chante?" Leo asked with concern, "If you're exhausted, I can take you home right now…"

"No… no… no… please, it's just something I remembered suddenly. It's not important really…not anymore…" Chante replied.

"I'm glad…" Leo replied back, noticing the resolute thrust of her chin and the beautiful eyes that wanted to reassure him everything was fine.

They drove for another fifteen minutes. New York traffic wasn't so bad. Leo drove to a café that was set back against an arbor of trees in the background. It was a quieter part of town. There were a few cars parked along the side of the road.

"This is where I usually go when I want good food. Their barbecued ribs are to die for." Leo informed her.

They entered a cozy bar with wooden tables spread across the interior. The wall lamps cast a soft glow across the dimly lit room. There were a few people around having a late dinner. Soft piped- in music added to the warm atmosphere of the restaurant.

Leo chose a table further away from most of the diners. Chante was elated, but again, she didn't understand why.

A waiter approached and Leo ordered for both of them. Chante was glad he did that. It felt like he was in charge of everything… and that made her feel pampered, like he knew what pleased her.

After the waiter had gone, Leo inched forward, positioned both elbows on the table, crossed the fingers of his hand, and rested his chin against them. He looked straight at her without saying a word.

Chante found his gaze made her self-conscious as she swept away an imaginary hair to the back of her ear.

"Enchanting Chante…," he murmured under his breath but loud enough for her to hear.

"Tell me all about you," he coaxed her.

And for the first time in a very long while, Chante felt her heart beat again. She tried not to put too much meaning into his words, but somehow Chante knew this guy was different. He was kind, caring, sweet and thoughtful. So different from…

But Chante didn't want to go there just now. In fact she was determined to move on and away from that memory. And the man in front of her appeared to want to come along to wherever her journey had begun.

59

Chapter Two

"So…is it a hot date?" Markey insisted after his sister had been silent for a few minutes.

"Uhmm…yes…its Leo Cadman. Remember him? He brought me home one night and you were still up," Chante reminded him.

"Oooh… the rock star? He's cool," Markey replied, remembering.

"He's not a rock star silly. He's an ER doctor." Chante corrected him.

Chante hadn't told her brother that she had been seeing Leo for some time now. After the late dinner, she wasn't expecting to see him again even if both worked in the same hospital. She didn't want to raise her expectations and be disappointed again. But during that particular night, Leo proved to be a good listener.

Chante found herself telling him about her early years, the succession of foster homes before she was finally adopted by the Greens, Markey's unexpected arrival into their lives, her parents' death, and her struggles in coping with Markey's ALS.

Leo wasn't only a good listener, but he was funny too. Chante found herself laughing over his experiences before he decided to become a doctor. He confided that he found his true calling working at the ER. The hours were long, but the gratification was instant, he said. If he was instrumental in making a patient live another day, he was content.

He made no mention of a girlfriend and Chante didn't see a ring on his finger so she assumed he was single…and available. Again, she curtailed the optimism that was forming inside her chest.

He was true to his word and dropped her off at her place. Chante was pleasantly surprised when Leo asked if he could come in and see her brother for a little while.

Markey didn't say much as he reached out to shake Leo's extended hand. He was probably more taken aback to see a dark stranger inside their living room. Chante ushered him out the door shortly after.

"Thanks for tonight…" Leo said as he bent forward giving her a peck on the cheeks.

Chante's face turned red as a warm heat suffused her cheeks. She hurriedly closed the door and hoped he didn't notice.

Leo sent a text message the next day asking to meet for coffee at the hospital cafeteria. Chante thought, why not? The cafeteria was a safe place… it meant thirty minutes for a coffee break.

The problem with a hospital cafeteria is the presence of knowing eyes that tend to put more into something uncomplicated as having coffee. Chante returned to the nurse's station and was ribbed endlessly about the sexy doctor she had coffee with. She denied vehemently that there was more to it than that, but she couldn't deny the warm buzz that enveloped her the rest of the day.

She didn't hear from him for the rest of the week. Chante was torn between calling him and dropping by the ER.

"He's probably too busy…," Chante reasoned out.

"…or on extended shift…," she consoled herself.

"…or it's his day off…," she thought feeling slightly dejected.

"…or he is not interested in seeing me anymore…," Chante concluded.

So it was to her utter delight as she stood by the hospital sidewalk waiting for the bus that would bring her home, a silver-grey Lexus cruised its way to where she stood.

Leo Cadman was just as gorgeous as ever. The corn rows were gone… instead his head was a crown of frizzy hair that tumbled gently down the nape of his neck.

He had no explanation for his long absence and Chante didn't ask. She was just glad to see him again. They had dinner at the same café, and she received the same gentle peck on the cheek when he said goodnight.

They saw each other again for the next couple of days, caught a movie, went bowling, and had coffee at the cafeteria, almost every afternoon.

Chante didn't know what their relationship status was. Leo always seemed eager to see her and was warm and engrossed with her company. He never tried to put his arms around her or hold her hand, which confused Chante incessantly. Did he like her or not. Was he just being a total gentleman? Should she make the first move to bring their relationship to the next level, she asked herself.

That was the reason she was in a state of confusion over the hot date tonight. She didn't want to seem too forward and be rejected. But she wanted to send the message across that she was open if he was interested.

Leo said he would take her dancing.

Chante settled for a little black mini dress that had a low neckline. She donned a pair of sheer stockings and high heeled shoes. She hoped he would find it sexy and not think she was going to a funeral.

Markey suggested she wore a gold bangle bracelet as her only accessory. She gathered her hair to the side in a messy chignon style and allowed the rest to fall softly across her shoulders.

"WOOT! WOOT!" Markey tweeted.

Chante was glad he approved as she stepped out of her bedroom.

The doorbell rang and Chante tried to stifle the nervous energy she felt.

Leo's face was a picture of dumbfounded surprise and appreciation. Frankly he had never seen her in anything but the ubiquitous hospital scrubs or jeans and a tee-shirt.

"You… you… you look ravishing Chante." Leo whispered.

Chante noticed the pupils of his eyes dilate. As they stepped out into the sidewalk to get to his car, Chante was alarmingly aware of his hand on her elbow that slowly slid downwards to hold her hand.

He took her to a posh ballroom dancing club in Long Island. The place was huge with round tables covered in white brocade cloth and an Ikea center piece lantern. The center of the room was hardwood floor that shone and reflected the lights of the lanterns on each table. A twenty piece orchestra was set back against one wall fronting the dance floor.

Chante felt like Cinderella. Leo chose a table for two and ordered a bottle of champagne. Holding the flute in her hand, Chante took a sip and immediately felt the bubbly go straight to her knees, turning them to jelly.

"I… I really don't dance, you know…" Chante confessed.

Leo gave her an enigmatic smile but said nothing. He seemed perfectly content watching the other couples dance The Swing, Cha-cha, or Tango their way around the ballroom.

Chante felt a slight disappointment. She would have loved at least to try it. Maybe they were here just to watch.

After a short break, the orchestra signaled the start of another piece. As the trumpet signaled the opening strains of "Moonlight Serenade," Leo pushed back his chair and reached out his hand asking for a dance.

"I don't know how to dance…" Chante repeated.

"Follow my lead…" Leo replied.

Chante walked with him to the dance floor. He held her right hand with his left and wrapped his other arm across her waist drawing her near. Chante stumbled in her haste to follow his lead. His proximity was giving her anxiety.

"Close your eyes and listen to the music… let me do the rest…" He whispered in her ear.

Chante did as she was told and relaxed. The music was poignant and very arousing. He was a smooth dancer. The arm across her back felt hot against the fabric of her dress. His thigh prodded hers towards the direction where his next step would lead them. Chante caught his rhythm and realized she could dance.

His groin would touch hers inadvertently and Chante had to control the impulse to gasp as she felt the firmness of what was inside those pants. She felt what she thought was the touch of his lips on her neck just above her shoulder. But she wasn't sure if it was a kiss. She realized she was thinking too much and decided to just lose herself in the music.

Leo brought her hand that was in his towards the back of his neck. He then lowered his own arm to join the other arm that was around her waist. Chante felt him draw her even nearer to him as she lifted her face to his. The look in his eyes told her what she needed to know.

He felt something and it was exactly what she was feeling too.

The rest of the dance was a blur in Chante's mind. Both were consumed by a primal urge that needed to be satisfied. When the music ended, Leo paid the bill and they were soon inside his car. Without a word spoken between them, he started the engine and drove like his ass was on fire.

They ended up in his apartment, and as soon as the door closed behind them, he pressed her against the wall, his eyes never leaving hers, his breath panting against his half-opened mouth. With the wall on her back and his entire body pressed tightly against hers, Chante felt his cock through the thin fabric of her dress. She wiggled her hips slightly allowing her crotch to feel him.

Leo's lips traveled down her neck and towards her ear. She could feel his warm breath as he gently bit her on the earlobe. His hands groped for her breast as he slowly stroked her hardened nipples.

Chante's hands caressed the back of his neck as she tried to pull him closer. Every inch of her skin yearned to be caressed by his lips. She could feel the strong beating of his heart as her hands feverishly tried to open the buttons of his shirt. She fondled the front of his pants and felt the hardness of his penis.

Leo pulled her towards the bedroom and undressed her slowly before taking off his clothes. Chante could hardly breathe as she stared at his naked body. The mat of dark pubes formed a triangular pattern against his groin. He picked her up in his arms and carried her to bed. He proceeded to kiss her lips before he followed a path down to her breasts, the side of her waist, down to her navel, her thighs, knees, and then her feet.

He planted himself between her legs and opened her thighs slowly. Chante was on fire as she felt his fingers slide between her labia and caressed her clit.

"You are so beautiful," he whispered huskily.

Chante felt the exact moment his tongue went down on her. Ice and fire shot through her entire being as he flicked his tongue on her protruding clit over and over again.

Her moans filled the room as Chante clawed the sides of the bed. She angled her hips upward to allow him more access to her cunt as she resisted the urge to cum.

Chante wanted Leo inside her mouth so she could taste him and savor the feel of his cock between her lips. She twisted around to set her free and pushed him to the bed.

Chante straddled Leo and allowed her fingers to play with one of his nipples while running her tongue against the other. Then she lowered herself slowly until his penis was within inches from her mouth. She grasped him with both hands as her tongue played with the tip of his bulging member.

Chante heard his rattled breathing as she slowly sucked his penis inch by inch, until he was completely inside her mouth. She bobbed up and down his entire shaft, sucking and caressing him.

Leo reached out and pulled her up by the waist and positioned her legs between his face. Her cunt was a few inches from his mouth. Chante felt him slide open the lips of her vagina and caressed her with his tongue. Both proceeded to devour each other relentlessly.

Chante knew from Leo's grunts that he was about to come. With arms and legs entwined, Leo set her down and positioned himself on top of her. Without losing a beat, he thrust his penis into her wet pussy and rammed into her repeatedly until they both shuddered in an orgasmic frenzy.

Leo lay spent and breathing heavily, nestled in Chante's arms. She reached out and caressed the sinewy muscles in his back. She knew she had feelings for this man, but didn't know how deep it went. She had been thinking about this time, when it would happen, where, and what she had to do to get there.

Instinctively, she realized that Leo was the kind of guy who would love honestly and give the relationship all that he had. He did not seem the kind of guy who went for casual sex. Chante wondered what she truly felt about him. His detachment these past few weeks challenged her; it confused her about him. Maybe that was the reason she made herself attractive tonight. See where it would lead to.

But was she getting ahead of herself? He hasn't said anything yet.

Until…

"I love you, Chante…I think I have loved you since the day I first met you." Leo said.

Chante was stunned. Really? Was that possible?

And then she remembered Jared and how easily she fell in love with him, how much she went through to get over her feelings for him.

"Would you like us to see each other exclusively?" Leo added after she remained silent.

"You mean the boyfriend-girlfriend thing?' Chante asked with a slight smile on her lips.

"I don't do the boyfriend-girlfriend thing…" Jared's words echoed in her mind.

"Yeah…would you like that…? I mean…" Leo asked, unsure if she was laughing at him.

Chante knew that she must cross the line somewhere. She vowed to get over Jared Lowell and Leo was everything Jared Lowell was not.

"Yes…I think I'd like that…very much." Chante answered.

Leo shifted his body and cradled her in his arms.

"I'm glad…I won't ever do anything to hurt you, Chante. That's a promise." Leo said.

Chante's mind rejoiced over those words, but she wondered why her heart was not exactly jumping for joy.

Time…that was all she needed, she thought.

Sometimes it takes the heart longer to accept. But she knew she had a good thing going with Dr. Leo

Cadman and she would be so foolish if she allowed her heart to rule her head and listen to that little voice telling her otherwise.

Chapter Three

"Damn…" Chante muttered under her breath as she erased an error on the application form on her desk.

She never realized how tedious it could be to answer everything in triplicate. The Board of Trustees of NY General Hospital needed every bit of information about her background… her parents, brother Markey, her entire life history, before she could be considered a candidate for scholarship.

Today was the last day of loan form submissions required by the Hospital Fund Trustee Board and she was rushing to catch the 5:00 pm deadline.

She considered herself lucky the hospital offered such scholarship grants for Certified Nursing Assistants wanting to become Registered Nurses.

She had spent the last few days searching for a school that had a bridge program. She found a community college that had a remaining slot, and she grabbed the opportunity. Then it was another stressful three days gathering the requirements for admission at the school.

Nurse Betty was happy over her decision and furnished her with a document on her Current Employment as a Certified Nursing Assistant. She had a good working history with the hospital, Nurse Betty said.

She couldn't find her CNA Training Certificate until Markey suggested that she look in their mom's papers. It was there among old photos of her as a child. She went back to her old school and asked for a photocopy of her GPA and realized she did really well in high school.

Now all she needed was to pay the admission fee and she would be a nursing student once more. She sincerely hoped the hospital would release the funds for the scholarship immediately.

Chante inspected the hospital forms and hoped she didn't miss anything important. Nurse Betty said Director Whittle was a stickler for protocol and would probably call her within days after she submitted the loan forms.

She was glad it was over with. She had missed out on meeting up with Leo these last couple of days. She knew he understood how badly she wanted this. He said he was supporting her all the way.

"It's all in the hands of the trustees now…" Chante said to herself as she plucked out her cell to call him.

"Hey babe…" Leo's cheerful voice greeted her.

Chante realized how lucky a girl she was to have him as a boyfriend. He was caring, thoughtful, and so sweet. The other nurses were all green with envy. Apparently, a lot of them had a secret crush on the good-looking doctor from the ER.

They constantly wheedled her about their dates, asking her to spare no details. Chante just laughed over their endless curiosity. He was hers… eat your hearts out… that's all they needed to know, she said.

"We can meet up after your shift," Chante told him over the phone, "I'm done and free and yours for the night."

"Great…" Leo answered, "See you at the lobby, uhhm around 7:00?"

"Ok, see you then…" Chante replied as she felt her phone buzz. She had a text message.

The message was short. It informed her to be at the 7th floor in ten minutes for the Trustees Board interview.

"That was quick," Chante thought.

She made her way up the banks of elevators, entered a lift and pushed the button for the 7th floor. She hoped that Director Whittle wouldn't take too long with the interview. This was just supposed to be standard procedure before a loan was released.

The seventh floor hallway had plush carpeting and was lined with doors announcing the names of the members of the board. Chante headed towards the end where she knew Director Whittle had his office.

A secretary greeted her with a smile as she pushed the door open.

"Chante Green to see Director Whittle," Chante announced.

"Oh…Director Whittle is on leave," the secretary informed her.

"But… but… I just got a text message asking me to come up here. I assumed it was for the forms I submitted earlier…about the scholarship grant…" Chante replied with some confusion.

"That's right," the secretary informed her, "please enter through that door."

Chante walked gingerly towards the closed door. If Director Whittle was not available then she was meeting someone else. Possibly another member of the board, she thought.

Chante turned the knob, opened the inner door and entered. The occupant was on a swivel chair with his back facing her. She glimpsed a stack of forms that the figure was holding in his hands.

Chante cleared her throat and said, "Err…my name is Chante Green and I was asked to come?"

The figure slowly pivoted around to face her and Chante let out a surprised gasp.

Jared Lowell was seated in the chair.

"Jared… err…I mean… Mr. Lowell…Uhmm… there must be a mista…" Chante managed to stammer.

And then she remembered.

Shit!!!

Jared Lowell was the biggest contributor for the trust fund. He probably owned the whole goddamn thing.

"Hello Chante," Jared greeted her coolly.

Chante was taken aback by the greediness of her eyes as she drunk in his appearance. He was in a three piece pin-striped suit that only managed to enhance the cobalt blue eyes. The longish hair definitely needed a haircut as it framed the patrician face.

"Well…don't just stand there. Take a seat." Jared instructed her.

Yup… still domineering, Chante thought as she urged her feet to move.

She felt an overwhelming desire to explain why she fled from him that day on the roof deck until she realized that she was not here for that. She was here because she needed money from him… from the board… so she can study to become a nurse.

She also realized the irony of her situation. He offered to keep her in a condo, buy her "stuff" which she refused. And now this?

Jared was studying the forms he held in her hand. His face was inscrutable.

"Jared, I understand if you…if the board denies my request…" Chante began.

"I'm granting it to you…" Jared said simply.

"What…?" Chante asked in bewilderment.

"The loan that you need… I'm granting it to you. There's no need to ask the board. I'll take care of it," Jared explained.

"Thank you…" Chante whispered almost on the verge of tears.

An uncomfortable silence followed. A silence that neither one knew how to fill.

"Why didn't you tell me your brother had ALS?" Jared inquired after some time.

"I… I… it just never came up, I guess," Chante replied.

Was that the reason he was being so nice to her? Because he pitied her?

Chante wanted to leave the office. Her sanity couldn't stand another second being near his presence.

"Thank you, again…I have to go…," Chante stammered as she rose from her chair.

"I'll walk you down. I'm on my way out too…" Jared replied rising from his chair.

Chante walked stiffly beside him towards the elevator. Really? This timing sucks, she thought.

The elevator doors swished shut and Chante felt the need to breathe. She didn't realize she was holding it in.

The gears of the lift seemed to grind ever sooo slowly as Chante counted the floor buttons flashing on the panel.

Sixth floor… fifth floor…fourth floor…

Chante was increasingly aware of Jared's presence in the confined space.

Third floor…Second floor…

"Would you like to have dinner with me?" Jared suddenly asked as the door opened to the lobby.

"What…?" Chante asked in sudden surprise.

"Oh... there's my girl," Leo's voice suddenly greeted them.

He approached them as Chante stayed rooted to the spot. He placed an arm across her shoulder proprietarily and drew her close.

Jared stood still, taken by surprise.

"Err…Leo…this is Jared Lowell. He just granted me the loan…Jared, this is Dr. Leo Cadman," Chante made the awkward introduction.

The two shook hands, Leo effusively, Jared stiffly.

"On behalf of my beautiful girlfriend, I'd like to say thanks. She is most deserving. Aren't you babe?" Leo declared giving Chante a tender look.

"I'm sure she is…" Jared replied coldly.

Chante watched as Jared turned to leave. She wanted to stop him… to explain why Leo's arm was across her shoulder… to ask if she heard right about him asking her out to dinner…or if she heard wrong.

But his receding figure left her with no options except to follow Leo out into his car. He was her boyfriend. He was so happy for her. And she should be too. But why did she feel so shitty instead?

Chapter Four

"What's wrong with you today, Chante?" Nurse Betty looked at her with irritation.

This was the second time she got the meds mixed up for a different patient. Her mind was spinning and she needed to focus, keep her composure, before Nurse Betty threw her out into the street.

But how could she?

Jared Lowell was in the same building, more appropriately, sitting in an office on the 7th floor, running the operation for the trust fund in the absence of Director Whittle.

Chante decided now was a good time to take a break. She wanted to gather her composure before returning to the floor. She needed her head straight before she accidentally murdered a patient.

She tried calling Leo's cell but the conversation was short. He was dealing with an emergency situation and couldn't join her for coffee.

She replayed in her mind the earlier exchange with Nurse Betty.

"Isn't that grand of him…donating his time to this hospital when he has so much to do?" Nurse Betty said in a voice that sounded like a swoon.

"You're such a lucky girl… you didn't need to face the whole board… and to get your loan in a matter of minutes? That's never happened before," Nurse Betty added.

Chante knew she shouldn't let this affect her. After all, there were five floors between them. There was no need to bump into each other by accident. She just needed to overcome the nervous tension in the pit of her stomach that was driving her insane.

Determined to concentrate more on her job, Chante returned to the Nurses' station.

"Oh…there you are," greeted Nurse Betty, "I received a call from HR. Seems like they need someone to help Mr. Lowell with all the records. I thought you might like the idea… this being a way of saying thanks for the fast release of your loan? So… I volunteered your services."

"WHAT???" Chante replied, horror written all over her face.

"What's wrong?" Nurse Betty asked, seeing the look on her face.

Chante realized she was in a no-win situation. She couldn't say no. That would make her look ungrateful. Besides, what reason could she possibly come up with for denying the request? She placed all her reserves foolishly on the five floors that were between them. But she was about to be thrown into the lion's den.

"Of course… of course… I'll do it…" Chante replied and hoped the supervisor wouldn't ask for an explanation over her initial reaction.

"Good…" Nurse Betty replied before turning back to her charts.

It was with trepidation that Chante entered the elevator on her way to the 7th floor. She glanced at her reflection on the mirrors lining the elevator wall. She wished she had the time to fix her hair or have a tube of lipstick to apply on her nude lips.

She pinched her cheeks hoping it would give her the rosy glow she wanted and realized there was no need. Her face was flushed. The thought of being near him again was unsettling. She shook her head to drive away all apprehension.

"This is work," she muttered to herself, "that's all it is…"

Jared was on the phone when she entered the office. The room was in disarray with folders and documents strewn all over. He stopped momentarily when he saw her and waved her in.

Chante didn't know whether to stand or sit. She looked at the mess on his desk and thought she should start organizing. But again, he may have done that purposely and she didn't want to create more chaos than what was already there.

"Mother says hi. She's delighted to know you're here to help…" Jared said, putting down the phone.

"Oh… oh… that's great. I hope she's feeling better," Chante replied.

Jared appeared to be all business and Chante was thankful. He told her how he needed organizing to be done, by alphabetical order, he said.

Chante went through the stacks of folders and started to file them. She wished she could do it outside by the secretary's table but it would seem silly if she brought them all out and bring them inside one by one, after she was done.

Truthfully, she wanted to be away from those eyes that followed her every move as she bent down, retrieved papers, and added them to the pile she had started.

She was about to pick up another set of papers that was on his table when he reached out his hand to stop her.

"Leave that…" he said.

Chante was stunned by the effect of his hand touching hers. She felt that familiar tingle that made the hair on her skin stand on end, like she touched an open socket.

She drew her hand away in an instant.

Jared scoffed and said, "Not so impervious after all…"

Chante decided the best defense was silence. She had nothing to say. He was right. She was just as affected now as she was when they first met.

"Tell me about that guy in the lobby. I assume he is
your boyfriend? And a doctor too. Not bad Chante
Green, not bad at all." Jared said.

Chante felt the hackles rise at the back of her neck.
Was he mocking her? Did he mean she was not worth a
doctor's attention?

She turned her back and started walking towards
another pile of papers.

She faked a drool and said, "Yes, Leo is my
boyfriend. He is the sweetest man I've been with and
the best lover I've ever had. I'll marry him if he asks."

There…that should put him in his place, she
thought. She turned around to get more documents and
ran smack into him.

Jared's sardonic smile was plastered all over his
face as he placed his arms around her waist and pulled
her close. Chante was taken by surprise at the sudden
proximity and gasped.

"Are you sure about that, Chante" Jared asked as he
lowered his face down to hers.

"Jared… please…," Chante whispered as his face
kept coming closer and closer.

She remembered the warmth of his lips on hers. She
remembered what his tongue could do to her. It could
make her forget her name.

"I could take you here on the table and you wouldn't
say no…" Jared taunted her.

"Jared… please…" Chante begged.

She was unsure if she was begging him to stop or to do as he pleased. Everything was so confusing.

"What do you want me to do… kiss you perhaps?" Jared asked, his lips almost upon hers.

Chante wanted to say no, she wanted to resist him. But her body was completely disconnected from her mind. This was so wrong, her mind was telling her. But her body had taken over completely as her lips said… "Yes."

Jared lips felt like the heat of a torrid dessert. His hands moved to each side of her face and clasped her, his lips feverishly parting her mouth. Then his tongue was inside her, probing, seeking, and demanding to be familiar with him once again.

Chante felt all her senses respond to his authority. She was helpless to deny him what she knew she wanted to give without restraint, without question for any repercussions. She knew that this was where she wanted to be.

"Oh Chante, what are you doing to me…?" Jared sighed against her lips.

Chante was breathing heavily as she pushed away from him. This time she had no intentions of fleeing from him. She wanted to confront this situation head on. This was unacceptable. Leo was in her life now. She couldn't stand the thought of hurting him. He didn't deserve it. Leo Cadman was everything she ever wanted in a man.

Or was he?

Jared saw the play of emotions as it crossed her face. He knew exactly what she was thinking.

He wanted her badly. He wanted to fuck the hell out of her. He tried to forget her during all these months but found it impossible. Every girl he dated, he found wanting. The skin was the wrong color, the eyes were not green enough, and the hair was too short or too long. He morphed these women in his mind to look like Chante. But he was never satisfied.

When the chance presented itself, he grabbed at the excuse of working with the board for the trust fund here at the hospital. Even his mother approved of the idea.

Director Whittle was pleased, of course. He wanted to go on vacation and the presence of the biggest contributor would boost the finances of the hospital. Money would come pouring in. Jared Lowell's presence and influence would ensure that it did.

Jared wasn't a guy who flaunted his emotions publicly. To the world, he was this cool, slick, unfeeling, rich sonofabitch. Women found that irresistible. He discovered early that women were easily blinded by his wealth and good looks. There was no shortage of skirts who gladly threw themselves into his arms. He didn't care if they loved him or not. He never invested his heart in any one before. His money made up far more than what he was not willing to give.

But Chante was different. This was the first time any woman had ever turned him down. That confused him because he knew she was sexually attracted to him.

That was pretty obvious after what happened between them the first night they met.

What did he say or do wrong that day on the roof deck to make her run away from him? That hurt him more than he cared to admit. He thought he was doing the right thing. That was the way he maneuvered all his past relationships.

When he saw her again last night, he was assailed with conflicting emotions. He felt an immense desire to take her into his arms and kiss her then. But he was afraid she'd run away again. So he played it cool.

Meeting that man, that Dr. Leo Cadman, at the lobby was unexpected. The way he put his arm across her shoulder like he owned her... he wanted to hit him right then and there. The way he looked at Chante like she was the most precious thing in the world. That annoyed him.

The thought that Chante went home and made love to him last night tormented him. He was intelligent enough to recognize that he was jealous. But he denied it vehemently. Jealousy was not supposed to be in his nature. How could it be? He never gave his heart away before.

He checked out Leo Cadman's record and found it outstanding. There was nothing he could fault him with. He found that very exasperating.

And now, he recognized all these thoughts in Chante's face. She was thinking of Leo Cadman and that made him feel cold all over.

Didn't she just kiss him back like he, Jared Lowell, was all that mattered to her?

Jared struggled with all these confusing emotions. One thing was certain. He wanted her to be around him long enough to unravel all the confusion that assaulted him.

"I'm sorry Chante. That was uncalled for. I think I missed you. Please don't run away again. I promise nothing will happen that you do not approve of." Jared said by way of explanation.

That was unexpected, Chante thought. Jared Lowell offering a truce was not something she saw coming.

"Ok…" Chante replied, hesitant yet appreciative for his concern.

That was a good start. She couldn't imagine what the next few days would be like if she had to resist him every time he made his advances. She knew she wanted that too, but there was Leo…

They spent the next few hours in easy camaraderie. Jared could be a joy to work with if he wasn't being the domineering person he was so used to being.

Chante found the hours flew by very fast and soon it was time to go.

"I assume the boyfriend is waiting for you at the lobby?"Jared teased her as she was preparing to leave.

"Yes…" Chante replied, suddenly realizing she was not looking forward to seeing Leo tonight at all.

"Well…ok then… let's not keep him waiting…" Jared replied.

Chante couldn't figure out the emotion she heard in his voice. Was he teasing her again? Why did he sound like he wasn't glad about that? She wanted to tell him that she'd rather stay here with him now, but the uneasy truce between them was so new. She didn't want anything to spoil it.

Chante hoped he would at least walk her down again to the lobby. She'd be happy just to have a precious few minutes more of his company.

But Jared turned away and made a move to pick up more documents on the table.

Chante felt a lump of disappointment in her throat. 'How easily he could dismiss her presence,' she thought.

She rode down the elevator feeling morose.

Leo was there waiting for her just as she thought. He was happy to see her again after missing out on their coffee break date.

He gave her a warm hug followed by a short passionate kiss. A few other nurses loitering about the lobby looked their way. Chante thought she saw envy in their eyes.

She should be feeling on top of the world, she mused. But she was assailed by guilt that was hard to explain. She tried her best to make her greeting at least sound as enthusiastic as he was.

"I've got a surprise for you," Leo whispered in her ear.

He ushered her out into his car that was parked by the sidewalk, opened the car door, and let her in.

Chante glance upward into the hospital building and thought she saw the silhouette of Jared outlined against one of the glass window of the 7th floor. Chante was sure he could see them from that window above.

Leo entered the car and revved up the engine. Soon they were cruising down the streets of New York City.

"Where're we going?" Chante inquired.

This wasn't the route home.

"You'll see when we get there," Leo answered mysteriously.

There was a noticeable gleam in his eyes as he reached for her hand before bringing it to his lips to kiss it. They drove in comfortable silence until they reached the café where they first had dinner.

"What could possibly be surprising about having dinner here?" Chante thought.

They have been here a couple of times more since that day.

The maître'd ushered them towards the rear of the café and out again through the back exit and into the darkness beyond.

"Leo…" Chante resisted at the hand that was pulling her forward.

She couldn't see anything up ahead except for the encompassing darkness.

Suddenly the darkness was illuminated by hundreds upon hundreds of glowing white bulbs. The trees were festooned with string lights bathing the place with an ethereal glow. It looked magical. And just beneath one of the trees was a table setting for two. A bottle of champagne nestled inside an ice bucket on top of the table.

"Oh Leo, this is so beautiful…" Chante cried out in wonder.

This was so typical of Leo… always trying to make her feel extra special.

"What are we celebrating tonight? Have you been promoted to ER Chief? What?" A clueless Chante asked.

Leo made a move to get something from his back pocket as Chante looked up at the trees around them.

When she glanced back at him, Leo was down on one knee. He held a small square box in his hand. He snapped the lid open, and without moving his eyes from her, took a small ring from inside the box and held it up for her to see.

Chante thought she was dreaming as she saw Leo holding up the ring and heard him say the words.

"I love you, Chante and I want to spend the rest of my life with you. Will you give me the honor of being my wife?" Leo said.

Chante was stunned beyond belief. This wasn't what she expected tonight… Leo down on his knees asking her to marry him. This was her dream after they seriously started dating one another. He was her dream come true. Dr. Leo Cadman was every girl's dream come true.

And here he was before her now, down on one knee, his face filled with promise to love her forever, and holding an engagement ring in his hand.

But why was she having difficulty seeing all that? Why was she seeing the face of Jared Lowell instead?

-To be continued in Book 3-

Book Three

Chapter One

IT HAS been three weeks since the marriage proposal and Chante knew what she had to do. She knew it since the night she said 'yes' to Dr. Leo Cadman. Her sense of right and wrong had been bothering her like crazy since. It wasn't like she didn't have feelings for Leo. In her heart there was a special place for him. Even her common sense was telling her she did the right thing in accepting the ring. But how could she deny the little nagging voice telling her she was a fraud?

If it were just her and Leo in the equation, the conclusion would be a given. There was no doubt that he was the perfect man for her. She could learn to love him totally. But the existence of one Jared Lowell made the equation more complex than it should have been.

Considering that Jared hasn't even hinted about his true feelings- or any feeling for that matter- about her, Chante thought she was awfully stupid to feel guilty about accepting Leo's marriage proposal.

Couldn't she just consider Jared an infatuation and move on with her 'happily ever after' with an eligible doctor who obviously was crazy in love with her?

She knew the answer. If she was really honest with herself, she knew it all along. It wasn't like a bolt of lightning that just came out of the blue. She was in love with Jared and she had to tell Leo the truth. Whatever the consequences or outcome about her decision, she had to do it soon.

The engagement ring he had given her lay heavily in her left hand ring finger. She shouldn't even have worn it out onto the streets. The single solitaire diamond reflected the light from the street lamps she passed by.

She spotted a small café, entered the premises and sat at a barstool. The bar of the café faced a glass mirror looking out into the street. It was a small dive compared to the more glitzy ones but it was in Queens and near the home she shared with her brother, Markey. His sleeping meds had taken effect almost immediately and Chante took the time to go out into the fresh air and think about her dilemma.

Droplets of rain cascaded down the glass window as Chante let out a sigh of frustration.

"Swell…" she muttered under her breath.

Even the weather was a reflection of the guilt in her heart. It was a good thing Leo was gone for the entire week. He had to attend a medical conference in Atlanta, giving Chante precious time to work out how she would handle the situation when he came back. Initially he was hesitant to leave so soon after the proposal. He wanted to spend as much time as he could with her but Chante reassured him it was fine. The medical conference was a step forward in his career as an ER doctor.

But even Chante understood why she wanted him away. It would give her time to put her thoughts into perspective and she could only do that if she wasn't feeling so guilty about him being around her all the time.

She had to break the engagement. It wasn't fair to the guy. How could she pretend to love him when she knew that her feelings didn't go deep enough to deserve the ring he had given her?

And Jared was gone too. He left word that he would be gone for a few days to attend to some personal concerns. That left Chante feeling gloomy and abandoned, but also relieved that he didn't have to know about her current status – engaged to Dr. Leo Cadman.

She was hoping that by the time Jared got back, if he ever came back at all, she would have untangled herself from this farce of an engagement.

Right now, she felt trapped between a rock and a hard place, but one thing was for sure, she had to break an engagement that she was sure she couldn't live up to.

She probably would end up alone and miserable just the same, but at least her conscience wouldn't be nagging her day and night.

Chante ordered a beer and nursed her drink. She glanced at her watch and decided to drink up and head for home. The rain was now just a drizzle and she could sprint the few blocks home.

She pulled out her purse to pay the bill when a familiar voice greeted her.

"Well-well-well, if it isn't my favorite girl. Fancy meeting you here." The voice sneered.

Chante whirled swiftly around, a sudden fear creeping into her heart. She knew that voice.

"Oh… hi Jimmy…" Chante addressed him with a squeaky voice.

The new arrival was Jimmy Derollo, her ex-boyfriend. The guy always gave her the creeps. Chante wondered what she ever saw in him. Even now as he sidled towards her in the bar, she felt her skin crawl and the hair on the back of her neck stand on end.

Their last confrontation weeks ago on the sidewalk while waiting for the bus was something Chante wanted to forget. The hard slap she gave him on the face after he tried to kiss her still resounded in her ear. She vaguely remembered the threat he made as she swiftly boarded the bus. But she couldn't forget the murderous look in his eyes as the bus pulled away from him.

The bar was half-full and Chante knew that Jimmy wouldn't try anything stupid. One scream and even the bartender would probably come to her rescue. Still…she wasn't sure if she could deal with him once she was outside the confines of the bar. He could follow her home and she came alone.

No…Chante decided her best defense was to play it nice. Maybe if she played her cards well, he would leave her alone.

"Jimmy," she said again as he took the barstool next to hers and coolly ordered a glass of beer.

Jimmy turned his head and eyed her. Chante was uncomfortable with the way his eyes travelled up and down her body. She decided to ignore it remembering that she needed to keep her wits about.

Jimmy took a slug from the mug that left froth around his upper lip. Chante fought the urge to cringe with distaste. The glint in his eyes scared her. But fear was one the things that she didn't want him to see. Guys like Jimmy Derollo were bullies and fear only made him more potent and dangerous.

"I'll cut to the chase, bitch…" Jimmy said in a low voice, "I need some money and you will give it to me."

"What?" Chante asked in shocked surprise, "what the fuck makes you think that I will give you…"

Her shock had turned to irritation and it showed in her voice.

"Oh…but you will," Jimmy replied in a cold voice, whipping out a cell phone from his back pocket.

Chante wondered what he meant and was confused. Jimmy was scrolling through his phone until he found what he was looking for.

"You and I…we made a movie together. You probably don't remember because you were fucking high out of your mind. But here…watch…," Jimmy said as he handed her the phone.

Chante took the phone from his hand as Jimmy pressed the 'play' button.

Chante watched in horror as the video ran. The position was moving unevenly as a hand held out the phone from a distance, but there was no mistaking the images in the video. It was her and Jimmy fucking the hell out of her. She knew she was unconscious when it was taken but anyone seeing it would think she had her eyes closed in ecstasy.

Chante dropped the phone as Jimmy caught it in his hand and placed it back inside his pocket.

"As I was saying…I need some money, or else…" He taunted her.

"Or else what…" Chante asked, the words coming out of her mouth with some difficulty.

"Oh you know… I could upload it to the hospital website. I'm sure the hospital bigwigs would be so happy to know that one of their nurses is such a slut." Jimmy said.

Chante was dumbfounded. She couldn't believe what she was hearing. He was blackmailing her with a video he took without her knowledge and she was helpless to do anything about it. She couldn't speak. The shock of seeing the images on the video turned her face gray with fear.

Suddenly her whole world was spinning around her. Everything turned black and she had to conquer the feeling of nausea that was threatening to overcome her. She grasped the edge of the bar to keep from falling.

"Jim-Jimmy, I-I-I'm not even a nurse…I'm an assistant nurse… and the little I earn go to the needs of Markey. You know that. Please-please, don't do this to me." Chante found herself begging.

She had a few bills in her purse and she felt
dismally pathetic as she scooped it out and handed it to
him.

Jimmy gave a chilling laugh as he pushed back her
hand. He was enjoying himself immensely.

"Stupid cunt, you think I will accept loose change?"
he asked.

And then he added, "You have access to the hospital
pharmacy, right? So…why don't you grab a few bottles
of them drugs and sell them to make money, right? A
few thousand…Or-or you can sell that ring on your
finger. Then your secret's safe with me."

Chante was horrified at what he was suggesting.

"Jimmy…that's impossible…I-I-can't do that." she
replied.

Jimmy stared at her as if she were the village idiot
who couldn't comprehend what he was saying. Then the
murderous look returned into his eyes.

"Fucking whore…I don't care where you get the
money as long as you get it, ok? Three days from today.
Or the whole world will see your juicy black pussy."
Jimmy whispered in her ear before he stood up and left
the bar.

Chante was rooted to the spot. Her heart hammered
wildly in her chest. She couldn't breathe as she dropped
a few bills on the counter and finally stumbled her way
out the exit.

"What have I done…" she whispered horrified.

She tried to remember as much detail of that particular night and realized her memory was too hazy. Jimmy must have known she never took drugs in all her life. No wonder she passed out cold. But the humiliation of just how low she had sunk filled her entire being.

She shivered as she made her way home. She couldn't open the door with her key. Her hand shook violently. She controlled the shiver that was engulfing her before she finally opened the lock. Once the door closed behind her, she felt an overwhelming sense of relief. At least she was safe inside her house.

Then just as suddenly, the enormity of her predicament struck her once more and she fell to the floor in a slump. Who could she turn too? She had no family except for Markey. She had no savings except for the salary she got as CNA and that wasn't much. It barely covered the rent and the groceries.

And even if she could get her hands on some money, will Jimmy hand over the video and forget everything?

Her brain shouted the truth of her predicament. There was no way Jimmy will ever be satisfied no matter how much money she could raise. He will use that to keep tormenting her until his attention shifted to something else.

Then what? A few weeks… or months later… before he shows up again? She could spend her whole life just being terribly afraid of him showing up again.

The hopelessness of her situation engulfed her once more. She had never felt more vulnerable and helpless her whole life. She cringed at the thought of the whole hospital finding out about her.

"Oh God…" Chante said in desperation.

Tears of helplessness and despair poured down her cheeks. She wished the ground would open up and swallow her whole. She had never felt more alone. Just when life was throwing her bits and pieces of hope, a dark past which she never expected have come to haunt her.

She struggled slowly to her feet and made her way to the bathroom. She felt an overwhelming desire to clean herself. She never felt so dirty in her entire life. Without even bothering to remove her clothes, she turned the shower on and stepped into the cold water. Her hair was wet and her drenched clothes stuck to her skin. But she knew that no matter how long she stayed inside the shower, it will never fully wash away the truth that she spent that one night in the arms of a scum bug like Jimmy Derollo.

Chapter Two

Chante forced her exhausted body out of bed the next morning. Dawn had broken the nighttime sky before heavy lids finally closed over tired eyes. She knew they would be red from crying, but there was nothing she could do about that now. She just hoped her brother wouldn't notice. She spent the whole night tossing and turning and thinking of a way out of her predicament.

Nothing proved to be the right solution. She knew that no matter where she went with this one Jimmy would always have the upper hand. He had the video and could extort money from her for as long as she lived.

She thought of moving away to escape him, but where would she go? Markey needed to be near a medical facility 24/7. And she was enrolled at the Community College and her tuition paid in full. If she suddenly disappeared, the hospital will definitely conduct a search. No…she had to stay and face the consequences.

She hoped and prayed that Jimmy would give her more time than the three days he threatened her with.

Chante felt the tears well in her eyes but she blinked them away. She couldn't afford to be weak. Not now…she needed to prepare Markey some breakfast and get ready for work.

She trudge into the kitchen in her bathrobe and realized that her brother was already up and in the living room watching cartoons.

"…morning," Markey greeted her.

"Hey…" Chante answered feebly.

She tried to keep her back to him so he wouldn't notice her red-rimmed eyes.

"What's wrong, Chant…" Markey inquired.

Chante didn't even realize he had wheeled himself from the living room and into the kitchen.

"What... oh… nothing… just a bad night, I guess." Chante evaded.

Markey said nothing but continued to watch her. Chante knew just how perceptive her brother was. She didn't want him to worry. She took in a deep breath and tried to put a huge smile on her face as she scooped some eggs and bacon onto his plate.

"Want some cereal to go with that?" She asked in a lighter voice.

Markey shook his head and started to eat. Chante poured herself a cup of coffee which she intended to bring back to the bedroom with her. She didn't want to sit at the breakfast table with him. She couldn't stand the thought of him seeing just how deeply troubled she was.

"Liza will be here shortly for your physical therapy," she announced to him.

"Ok…" Markey agreed and then added, "Chant, whatever it is, it'll be fine."

Chante was swept with an overwhelming desire to embrace him. She retraced her steps and placed her arms around him.

"Of course it will 'lil' bro…we will be fine. You and I both." Chante whispered in his ear.

Chante spent the next two days with her head in a swirling cloud of gray. It took all of her will to focus and concentrate on the things she had to do. She was glad that the hospital was full and she hardly had time to think about her situation. She moved about in a frenzy performing her duties, foregoing lunch, and she'd go straight home thoroughly exhausted and straight to bed.

She had formulated a plan. She would call Jimmy and ask to meet with him on the third day. Then she would beg him to give her some more time to come up with a substantial amount. If she needed to go down on her knees, she would. But the thought of seeing him again made her sick to the pit of her stomach. But that plan was the most she could come up with.

As the third day wore on, she found herself more and more nervous about what lie ahead. She realized that Jimmy would probably be waiting for her call and expecting that she had money with her. The thought made her nauseous. She ran to the toilet and slumped onto the bowl as bile regurgitated from the pit of her stomach. She heaved dryly. She hadn't eaten in almost three days. She splashed cold water onto her face and hoped that she looked none the worst for what was ahead.

As she trudged resignedly back to the nurses' station, she heard Nurse Betty call out her name. She held a stack of folders in her hand which she deposited into a satchel.

"Chante, I need you to bring this to…what's wrong? You look like you went through a meat grinder," Nurse Betty declared as she got a closer look at Chante's face.

"Bum stomach…" Chante lied.

"Are you alright?" the supervisor asked with concern.

"Yeah…I'll be fine…" Chante whispered weakly.

"OK…as I was saying, I need you to bring these documents to The Plaza. Mr. Lowell needs them ASAP," Nurse Betty informed her.

Mr. Lowell? Chante's senses fired up at the name. Jared Lowell? Was he back in New York?

Chante's equilibrium was sliced in half. Her heart managed to crawl out of its dark hole and celebrated the notion of seeing him again while her brain remained adamant, reminding her of Jimmy Derollo.

She took the satchel and reassured her supervisor that she knew where the plaza was. It was near Central Park and the streets were lined with recreational facilities and the boutique shops on Fifth and Madison Avenues.

When she reached the hotel, she headed straight to the reception area and asked to be directed to Mr. Lowell's room.

"It's the penthouse, Miss," the receptionist informed her with a look that said, 'did you really have to ask?'

"Of course it had to be the penthouse…" Chante mumbled to herself.

She glanced at her wrist watch and saw that it was 6:55 p.m. She would drop off the satchel and leave. The sooner she made contact with Jimmy the better. She didn't have any idea how he would accept her appeal, asking for a few days more.

The thought left her without sensation, foreshadowing whatever excitement she felt about seeing Jared again.

The elevator silently whisked her all the way to the top of The Plaza. She stepped out when it came to a stop and headed for the suite. She knocked at the Oakwood paneling of the Deluxe Rose Suite.

Jared opened the door and once again Chante was awestruck by the stunning beauty of the man. He must have just taken a shower because his hair appeared damp and disheveled. He was wearing a faded pair of Levi jeans and was shirtless. The six-pack rippled and glistened with moisture. The guy obviously had no need for a towel.

His brows knitted together and Chante thought he was not pleased to see her at all.

"Hi Jared…" Chante murmured as she awkwardly reached out her hand to pass on the satchel.

She averted her eyes from his half-naked body. She had no intentions of staying long or she would lose her mind completely.

"Chante…," his husky voice murmured her name, "Come in, please."

"I-err-I-I-can't s-s-stay…" Chante stuttered as Jared moved closer.

Chante stepped out of his way to avoid brushing against him as he closed the door behind her.

She expected the room to be pleasant but it was more breathtaking than she expected. The myriad lights of the New York skyline reflected against the glass windows of the living room.

Chante wondered why she always felt gauche in his presence. She felt like she had four sets of arms and legs and didn't know which limb to move first. She stayed rooted at the threshold as Jared sauntered towards the settee in the center of the room.

Chante prodded her feet to move forward. It seemed she had no choice except to stay a little while longer. She still held the satchel in her hand as she approached nearer.

"Nurse Betty said you needed this…so here…," Chante said placing the bag full of documents onto the table.

Jared sat down and gestured for her to do the same. He hadn't said another word since opening the door and the silence was starting to feel awkward. If Chante hadn't been so blinded by him, she would have noticed how his eyes lit up seeing her again. But it was her drawn and haggard face that immediately caught his attention.

Chante sat down tentatively only to rise again like her ass was on fire. She didn't want to inflict her presence on him.

"Sit down…," Jared ordered her softly.

There was no denying the command behind the softly spoken words. Chante sat down once again feeling like a marionette on strings. She clasped and unclasped her fingers and kept her eyes focused on her hands.

"Look at me…," Jared commanded once again.

Chante was compelled to obey. Emerald-green eyes locked with cobalt-blue ones.

"What's wrong," Jared asked softly this time. "You look like shit. Is that doctor of yours giving you trouble?"

"What?! Leo??? No-no-no…it's not about him…" Chante answered hastily.

"Your brother then…" Jared asked immediately.

"Markey? No-no-Markey is fine." Chante replied.

"Work?" Jared continued.

"No." Chante answered.

"Are we going to play 'Twenty Questions' or are you going to tell me what's wrong with you?" Jared sighed with exasperation.

Chante knew that Jared wouldn't stop until he flushed the truth out of her. But how could she even tell him about Jimmy and his extortion scheme? That video was the most horrifying thing that had ever happened to her and she had no intention of letting him know just how low she had sunk in the past.

Jared stared at her and saw the conflicting emotions pass through her face. He knew she was in some kind of trouble. Just as he knew it was something she was reluctant to share with him.

"Chante, listen…I know something's wrong. And obviously you are carrying this alone. You've lost a lot of weight. I see that. Let me help you…please. Whatever it is, I'm sure there's something I can do," Jared pleaded.

Chante was taken aback by the impassioned plea. She never in her wildest dreams considered Jared a shoulder to cry on. But the enormity of her burden during the last three days was suddenly too much to bear. Her shoulder slumped against the cushion as tears came rushing to her eyes. And like a dam that had been filled to overflowing, her sobs racked her body as her breath rattled against her throat.

"Hey…hey…hey…it's alright…," Jared said softly as he moved close beside her on the sofa and placed an arm across her shoulder.

Despite her distress, Chante was keenly aware of the fresh smell that permeated his body.

"No Jared, it's not alright…," She said between sobs.

Then she told him the truth. She kept nothing back. She shared with him about the lonely days after her mom passed away. Her confusion and fear about Markey. She told him about meeting Jimmy Derollo and the night he brought her to his apartment. And finally her humiliation over the video that Jimmy Derollo threatened to upload unless she came up with money tonight.

Throughout it all, Jared listened without saying a word. The only visible sign of his fury was a clenched jaw and the arm that tightened around Chante's shoulder.

"Are you… are you disgusted with me?" Chante asked in a hoarse voice.

Jared responded by taking her gently into his arms.

"Disgusted? No. Absolutely not. You were confused, lonely and scared and this bastard took advantage of you," Jared replied.

Chante nestled gently in his embrace. It felt so good to be in his arms. There was no other place she would rather be right this minute but she had to see Jimmy tonight and beg for an extension. She struggled out of his embrace, feeling immediately bereft, like coming from a warm bed and out into the cold.

"You're not going out to meet him tonight…I will," Jared said.

"But…," Chante replied confused.

"Give him a call. Tell him to meet you at the same bar and that you have the money with you. DO IT NOW!" Jared ordered her.

Chante was still confused but was compelled to do as he asked. When Jared spoke that way, she doubted anyone would ever try to cross him. Not even his mother.

Chante made the call as Jared threw on a shirt and a jacket.

"Stay here…wait for me till I get back…" Jared said quietly.

Chante was afraid of the look in his eyes. It had taken the color of an angry sea. His voice had a steely edge she'd never heard before.

"Jared, he might hurt you…," Chante protested as she clung to his arm in an attempt to stop him from leaving.

Jared grasped both her hands that were clinging tightly and held them in his own.

"I'll be fine, Chante. Stay here. I'll be back soon." Jared said before heading out the door.

After Jared left, Chante was collapsed in anger and desperation. She wanted to run after him, stop him from going to the bar. This was all so bad, she thought. The feeling of foreboding was so strong. And it was all her fault.

What she had done was manage to send Jared out to face an unknown danger. She should be the one out there, not him. This was her problem, not his. She never expected his reaction to be so quick.

"I should never have told him…," she thought.

"What if he gets hurt…or God forbid, even killed by Jimmy?" Chante muttered in agony.

How could she face his family? His mom…and dad…or girlfriend.

"Does he have a girlfriend?" Chante was momentarily sidetracked from her worry.

"He's been gone for so long...," Chante continued with her soliloquy.

She glanced at her watch and realized he had just been gone for twenty minutes and yet it felt like a lifetime.

She paced the floor, and then sat down on the sofa, only to jump up once more and continue with her pacing. She hardly noticed the plush surrounding, the rich texture of the upholstery on the chairs, the thick carpet on the floor, the luxurious colors on the wall, the fresh flowers strewn about the niches and crannies, and the beautiful artwork that hung all around the suite.

She hardly noticed any of these details yet the whole place screamed of the personality and character of someone like Jared Lowell. This place was who he was.

A far cry from her reality-penniless… a sick brother… struggling to make ends meet.

Who was she to him? An accidental fuck brought about by circumstances of her making? Would he have given her a second look back at his mom's hospital room if she didn't challenge his machismo? Taunting him to kiss her so she could tell the nurses what a lousy kisser he was?

She remembered his proposition up on the roof deck and the pain she felt. It wasn't because she thought he treated her like a whore... offering her material comforts that she could only dream of. No…it wasn't that.

Chante now recognized the reason. It was because she believed in the fairytale ending. The happily ever after from books she read as a child. She always did. She wanted him to offer her more than just the luxuries that came with his fortune, or her being his kept woman…his sex toy. She wanted everything… heart, body, mind, and spirit. They could live in a shoebox and she'd be happy just to be with him. She wanted his promise of forever.

With all these thoughts running through her mind, Chante was suddenly struck with excruciating terror. What if she never saw him again after tonight? If something happened to him out there, she wouldn't be able to live with herself. Tears welled up in her eyes once again. She felt an icy coldness creep from her heart and envelop her entire body as she shivered violently.

If she could only turn back the hands of time, she would. It had been hours since he was gone.

She was so wrapped up in her desolation she hardly noticed the main door open silently.

"Chante…" Jared called out her name.

Chante stopped pacing and turned to where she heard his voice. She thought she was dreaming, her mind on overdrive. But no…it really was him, standing by the threshold.

"Jared?" she declared in a breathy unbelieving voice, still unsure if she was hallucinating.

Her knees turned to jelly as total desolation changed to encompassing relief. She swayed as the room spun around her.

From the corner of her eye she saw Jared take three large steps and caught her just before she lost her balance completely.

"Jared…oh God. Jared…you're back… you're back…thank God, you're back…" she cried out.

Without letting go of her, Jared led her to the sofa and sat down beside her.

Chante felt the need for reassurance that it was really him. She reached out her hand and touched his face.

"It's you…it's really you..," she muttered incoherently.

"Of course it's really me…unless you're expecting some else… then I can go…" Jared said seriously but the twinkle in his eyes belied the words.

The sound of his voice cleared all the cobwebs in her head. She had never felt more exhilarated and alive in her whole life. Jared was back.

And then Chante remembered why he left in the first place.

"What…how…did you…are you…?" the surge of questions rushing to her brain made the words difficult to form.

"If you promise me you're alright, then I'll tell you everything," Jared said calmly.

Chante nodded her head. She needed to keep calm if she were to get the whole story.

Jared took a deep breath and said, "I went to bar and waited for him. I didn't have to wait long. I recognized the scum bug the moment he entered. I asked him if he was waiting for you. He looked at me in surprise and said yes. I said you weren't coming and that I wanted something that he shouldn't have. And he gave it to me."

Jared reached into his pocket and drew out two objects.

"That's the hard drive to his computer and the memory card to his cell phone. Destroy it. And he promised never to get even remotely close to you again," Jared ended coolly.

Chante's eyes were wide as saucers. She couldn't believe what she was hearing. No way did things just happen the way he narrated it. There had to be more to it than that. She knew Jimmy Derollo… knew how mean and violent he could be. Jared wasn't telling her everything. She just knew it.

"Jar…," she began to protest.

But Jared placed a finger to her lips to stop her from asking more questions. He wasn't going to tell her anything more. She got that.

"That's all you need to know, Chante," Jared said firmly.

Chante slumped back into the backrest of the sofa. She couldn't believe her luck. The days of torment were over for her. Just like that. Then she remembered something. Her face suffused in shame and embarrassment.

"Did you see…," she couldn't even finish her sentence, the humiliation was overwhelming.

"No…I didn't want to. It's something personal that happened in your past," Jared answered with understanding.

Chante felt like she was submerged in cool cleansing water. She felt reborn and new. He gave her a new lease on the future. She didn't have to leave town, she didn't have to hide from anyone… her slate had been erased clean and it was all because of him.

Chante was filled with new hope. How could she ever repay him? There was no way she could ever equal what he had just given her tonight. He gave her back her life.

She raised her head up to give him a peck on the cheek. He was so close that all she had to do was inch her face forward. But Jared wasn't expecting that and turned towards her. And at that precise moment her kiss landed on his lips.

Jared stiffened at the unexpected intimacy. His adrenalin was still pumping. There was a lot he didn't tell Chante. He wanted to spare her the ugly details. But the unexpected feel of her lips on his unleashed all the pent-up control that built up since his encounter with Jimmy.

He pulled her close, and then even closer. His arms entwined around her waist with a viselike grip. Chante's arms snaked around his neck, her lips parting to allow his tongue entry. She felt his body emanating with a heat that burned and urged her to abandon all restraint.

Jared scooped her from off the sofa and carried her into the bedroom. Chante's heart was beating wildly, mesmerized by the thought of what was ahead. Chante knew she wouldn't hesitate. Not this time. This is what she wanted and her compliant body told him that.

Jared positioned her on the floor, their lips still pressed together, unable to let go. His fingers and palms were kneading and caressing her back as she felt the friction through the flimsy material of her clothes.

"Let me see all of you." Jared commanded.

And like a machine that animated under its master's power, Chante obeyed.

First she pulled out the barrette that was holding her hair and allowed it to fall softly against her shoulders. Her fingers moved and hovered tantalizingly on the hem of her blouse before she began to raise it up and over her head. Then she unzipped her pants and allowed them to drop carelessly around her ankles before kicking them aside. She stood before him naked except for her undies.

Jared's eyes drank in the tawny sheen of her light chocolate skin, the full breasts that begged to be set free from its confines, the narrow waist that angled softly to ample hips. He looked at her face and saw how her eyes dilated with desire, her lips parted, her breathing shallow.

He stepped closer and reached behind to unclasp her bra, setting free nipples that puckered hard with her lust. Chante shimmied out of her panties, exposing a trimmed bush of pubes.

He cupped both of her breasts, running his palms over the hard nipples, gently holding them in his hands. Her skin was as incredibly silky and soft as it looked, yielding instantly to his strokes, giving way to his insistent caresses. He kept stroking her, bringing his hands to the flat belly, and then to her back, sensing her shiver each time his fingers reached the firm swell of her ass, her breathing becoming more and more abandoned.

Jared brought her to the bed, slow, gently. He had to exert control not to fuck her there and then. He wanted this to be a slow dance, unlike their frenetic mating the first time they met.

Chante was bemused, dazed, her whole body ablaze. Her brain, which had detached from her body, watched in rapt attention as Jared removed all his clothes. She couldn't take her eyes off the throbbing cock that reared up with a life of its own. The thin skin on his cock shone with a pinkish hue while the head was suffused in a darker shade of crimson.

She was bewildered as he positioned her arms towards the back of the bed and pulled her body down near the edge of the bed. He spread her knees apart and guided one leg so that one foot was firmly planted on the floor.

Jared bent his head before her open thighs and felt the warmth even before he touched her. He parted the lips of her pussy, blowing gently against her clit, caressing them with his breath. Then his tongue reached out and began kissing her there. Chante moaned as her back arched with the anticipated pleasure. Jared gently kissing her clit was beyond her wildest imagination. She thought she had reached the zenith of her pleasure until he began sucking her. Chante bucked wildly as bolts of blue fire went shooting through her entire body.

She was already wet when they started kissing and now her juices were flowing freely from her pussy. Jared slipped a finger inside her, keeping his tongue firmly sucking on her clit. Chante thought she would surely go insane. She was moaning loudly, her back arched from the bed, her fingers clawing wildly at the headboard.

She wanted him to stop or else she would lose her mind as his fingers twirled inside her and his relentless tongue tortured her swollen clit. The muscles deep inside her vagina clenched around his finger desperately wanting his cock more than anything in the world but still unable to let go.

Chante was moaning as her body was racked with torturous hot and cold sensations. She didn't want to cum in his mouth and her hands groped wildly through his hair. But she knew she was losing all control of her body. She bucked wildly as Jared slowed down the circling motion of his tongue against her clit only to pick up speed once more, drawing her further away from the little that was left of her self-control. She felt her vagina spasm as she let out a keening cry of pleasure. Her body shook in one final arch before she collapsed onto the bed unable to contain her orgasm.

"Jared, I'm so sorry," Chante uttered breathlessly.

But Jared scrambled onto the bed and flipped her over. He pulled her by the hips until she was kneeling on the bed with her ass up in the air. Chante felt the head of his cock probing the opening of her ass before sliding down and entering her pussy from behind.

Jared reached out and cupped her breast, his thumb and forefinger twirling against her sensitive nipples. Chante realized the tension was building up once again inside her. Jared thrust into her slowly as his hands traveled down to her engorged clitoris. Chante almost jumped as a warm current passed through her whole body.

Her own cum had made her so slick that Jared had an easy time rubbing both sides of her hood between his fingers. He rubbed her slowly and then with ever increasing intensity as his thrust grew harder and stronger. Chante felt her orgasm building inside again. And as she climbed higher and higher into her own release, she heard Jared grunt like an animal in heat before she felt her own body start to shake. With one final thrust Jared came inside her as the muscles inside her cunt clenched violently before following with her own cum.

Chapter Three

In a seedy part of Queens, decrepit and broken-down warehouses lined an alley littered with garbage. Trash vats lay strewn all over the narrow cobblestone as rats scurried in and out of open bins in search of food scraps. A stench of death and decay filled the air.

One particular building had its door pried open. The marks of a crowbar were visible against the door jamb as the doorknob lay teetering and dented against the door.

A flight of stairs led to the second floor of the building where floorboards were broken and knawed away in several places. Rat droppings littered everywhere. A slight breeze blew against a torn and dirty curtain hanging by a glass pane, remnants of its shattered glass sticking out of the edges of the window sill.

A broken couch with its spiral coils showing through the tattered upholstery was positioned against the window. Whatever little light filtered through the glass was obscured by cigarette smoke that hung heavily in the air.

A stooped figure limped painfully towards the couch in small measured steps. Any abrupt movement triggered spasms of pain from his broken ribs. His entire body throbbed. He reached the sofa and lowered his ass down slowly. A neoprene wrist pad covered his left hand. He tried flexing his fingers to gauge the damage on the muscles and was instantly rewarded by a stab of pain that reached all the way to his elbow.

"Fuck…" Jimmy Derollo grimaced in pain.

He had been hiding in this dump for the last twenty four hours. He couldn't show himself back in the old neighborhood. The bruises on his face and neck would be a dead giveaway. Someone may just think of calling his parole officer, and then shit would hit the fan, that's for sure.

No…he'd burrow his broken body here in this dump and wait until he felt better. He had all the time in the world. His stash of crack cocaine and a bottle of brandy lay at the foot of the sofa. That should get him through for the next few days.

He remembered last night and what happened. He was waiting for Chante at the bar when this stranger came to him. He said that Chante was outside in his car with the money Jimmy needed. The guy opened the side of a black SUV and shoved him in. The next thing Jimmy knew he was punched kicked and pummeled to the floor of the car. He was beaten to within an inch of his life. Jimmy begged for mercy saying he had some money in his pocket and the man could have everything he wanted.

The guy smashed his head against the floor of the SUV and said that all he needed was the video he had of Chante. Jimmy got a clearer glimpse of his face. He thought he recognized the face but couldn't put a name to it. But it was the eyes that drove Jimmy to terror.

There was a look of murderous rage in them. Jimmy knew that if he didn't do as told, the stranger wouldn't have second thoughts ending Jimmy's miserable life.

Jimmy cowered in fear as he took his cell phone from his back pocket. The man removed the memory card and erased the video. Next they took a small drive to Jimmy's apartment where the man smashed his laptop and removed the hard drive from within.

Before he drove away the man hissed a message into his ear, "If you ever come near her again, I swear to God, no one will ever find your body," the guy threatened in a menacing voice.

Jimmy didn't even realize he pissed his pants till the car was out of sight. He went back into his apartment, gathered a few things and left quickly before the pain hit him hard.

Jimmy reached out for his stash and spread some white stuff on a piece of broken glass pane he retrieved from the window. He snorted hard and waited for the anesthetic effect to remove some of the pain. He took a swig from the brandy. With some of the pain gone, Jimmy managed to gather some coherent thoughts.

"That fucking bitch…this is all her doing… managed to hire a thug… paid money to get the video back. But how? She claimed to have no money… even fucking begged me not to do it. That guy…he looked familiar…not the kind of thug who'd do this for cash. I know him…I've seen him somewhere before." Jimmy sorted through his fogged brain.

And then in a moment of clarity, Jimmy straightened, triggering his broken ribs to press hard against his chest muscle.

"Awww…," Jimmy cried in pain.

"The Village Voice," Jimmy suddenly remembered a local newspaper, "some kind of announcement about a fucking director for NY General Hospital."

"Gareth…Jeric…Jared Lowell…that's it. That's the guy from last night. Fucking Jared Lowell, head of Lowell Enterprise. Well…well…well, looks like my Chante had gotten herself some fancy fuck." Jimmy said.

The pain wracking his body burned into slow anger. Jimmy fueled the anger by snorting more cocaine until the combined effects with the alcohol produced a blind rage. He forgot that he was under parole as a plan slowly formed in his head. When the scenario was executed perfectly in his mind, he slumped back slowly onto the sofa and closed his eyes.

A sinister smile marked his face as he muttered into the darkness, "We shall meet again Chante Green. And when we do, my face will be the last image you will ever see."

Chapter Four

Chante stepped down from the curb in front of the café. She refused to look back. She knew that the silhouette of Leo Cadman would be visible even from outside. His dejection was hard to bear. But Chante knew she did the right thing.

She determined that breaking up with Leo would be difficult. But it was harder to live with the guilt that hounded her every single day. Ever since the night she spent in the arms of Jared, she knew this time would come.

But she was wracked with uncertainty as well and that was not something she wanted Leo to see. When Leo asked her why, she didn't know how exactly to answer the question. But Leo was intuitive and when he asked if there was someone else, Chante nodded her head indicating he was right.

Chante was glad he didn't ask who. Her ambiguity rose from the fact that she didn't know where she stood with Jared. The time they spent together was something that she will forever remember, if memories were all that she would have. When she left that morning, Jared was still sleeping. She hurriedly scribbled a note thanking him for everything he had done for her.

Breaking up with Leo meant she had just blown her chances for a stable future beside a promising doctor and a man who obviously adored her. Chante had to convince herself that this decision had nothing to do with Jared. Whether he was in her life or not, she had to do the right thing. She wasn't in love with Leo, and that was the hard truth.

Jared had called her a couple of times since that night but Chante refused to take any of his calls. She was determined to set things straight with Leo before she even came near Jared again. She didn't want her conscience compounded with guilt of cheating on Leo every time she came near the presence of Jared Lowell.

But now it was done and Chante felt liberated for the first time since she accepted Leo's proposal. She wanted to call Jared but her insecurity about everything concerning him was brought to the forefront once again. She decided to wait for his next call…if he will ever call her again.

Her phone rang and Chante's heart leapt to her throat.

"Hey, Chant...," she recognized her brother's voice on the line

"Markey…is something wrong?" Chante asked trying to hide the disappointment in her voice.

"Nah…just wanted to say that you had a visitor a few minutes ago. He had the most awesome car. T'was a Benz. It had the most awesome panoramic glass roof. He took me driving around the block." Markey said with obvious excitement in his voice.

"WHAT??? You went driving with someone I don't know about?" Chante asked with horror in her voice.

"Well, he said you were a good friend. And he looked good. You know…real rich and all that stuff." Markey replied with a hint of regret.

"Besides, Liza said it was alright. I mean…she was all ruffled and confused and didn't know how to act around him. She was all red in the face like she was on fire or sumthin…" Markey informed her.

Chante knew that Markey was trying to deflect the attention from what he did. But a twinge of excitement began to bloom in her stomach.

"Did-did he say who he was?" Chante asked.

"Uhmm…said his name was Jared Lowell and that he works in the same hospital you do. That's why I thought it was ok. Are you mad at me for driving with him? T'was really cool…you know," Markey posed with some hesitation.

"Yeah…yeah…it's alright Markey. But don't you ever do that again without telling me first," Chante reprimanded her brother.

"Okay," Markey replied, "but Jared said that he's been calling you and you don't pick up the phone. So he looked up where you lived and all that stuff." Markey informed her.

"Did… did Jared say where I can find him?" Chante asked trying to hide the excitement in her voice.

"Yup…said he was goin' back to the hospital…" Markey answered.

Chante hung up the phone and hailed a passing cab. She wanted to get to Jared fast. If she had wings she'd probably be floating on air right now. Surely, him coming to her house… looking for her meant something. And he'd been calling her too.

The excitement in the pit of her stomach started to bloom. For some strange reason she felt exhilarated, euphoric, expectant. She was going to see him again. She told the cabbie to proceed to NY General as she sat back and tried to contain her excitement. She whipped out her compact mirror and stared at her reflection. Her eyes were luminous and her face was flushed. She hardly noticed the passing scenery, mentally urging the cab to go even faster. She breathed a sigh of relief as they turned a corner leading to the entrance of NY General.

She almost jumped out of the cab in her rush to see him. And she did. He was coming from the opposite direction. The disheveled hair flying in the breeze, the long strides of powerfully built legs wrapped in denim jeans, the white shirt with the sleeves rolled all the way to his elbow… all these images stamped their mark in Chante's psyche. His head was bowed as if he carried the world on his shoulders. Chante could see clearly the glumness that creased his face.

"Jared…," Chante called out.

Chante immediately saw the transformation on his face. He looked at her from afar like she was everything he wanted to see. The glumness gave way to relief that was followed by a smile of pure joy.

Chante ran to him like the devil was after her. She wanted to feel his arms around her… she wanted him to kiss her. She came to a full stop when she was right in front of him, suddenly feeling shy. She had to restrain herself. The lobby was full of bystanders and it was broad daylight.

They stood there in the sunlight. Jared's hands clasped her upper arms, her hands on his chest. They drank in the sight of each other. Their eyes devoured each other. Chante saw when Jared looked up past her head like something caught his attention. The silly grin that was on his face vanished and was replaced by surprise that suddenly turned into one of horror.

She swiveled her head halfway to see. And then she heard the voice.

"Bitch and your man-whore….," the slurred voice of Jimmy Derollo reached her ear.

Chante couldn't remember what happened next. Everything was a blur. She felt Jared yank her hard to the side and away just as two gunshots filled the air.

Pandemonium broke loose. People scampered everywhere. Screams filled the air. Chante thought she saw everything in slow motion… hospital security police rushing out and pinning Jimmy to the ground. The wail of a siren blared in the distance.

Chante looked at Jared and saw that the front of his shirt was stained with a crimson color.

Blood…blood…was the thought that came rushing into Chante's mind.

Jared tottered and Chante grabbed him just before he collapsed onto the ground.

"NO…GOD…JARED… NO!!! Chante recalled screaming at the top of her voice.

Jared reached out a bloodied hand to touch her face.

"I love you, Chante," he whispered before he slumped against her chest.

Chapter Five

The hours that followed the shooting of Jared Lowell were a blur in Chante's mind. Emergency personnel, doctors and nurses came rushing out of the hospital in droves. A trolley was speedily brought out from the emergency door as a mob of white-coated medics followed in hot pursuit. Instructions were shouted by a doctor and carried out by nurses before Jared was whisked back inside the hospital.

Chante stood numbed with shock. Her whole body had turned cold. She couldn't stop crying and screaming Jared's name. Nurse Betty and some of the other nurses from the second floor came and tried to calm her down. She felt a prick on her arm and realized she was injected with a sedative.

But she didn't want to go to sleep. She had to go and see what was happening with him.

"It's alright, honey, it's just for you to calm down." Nurse Betty declared.

Chante insisted on being brought to the ER. She almost got away from them before Nurse Betty got hold of her and told her she couldn't do that. Jared was being prepped for surgery.

She calmed down long enough for them to accompany her to the waiting room. That was the most they could do for her but Nurse Betty promised to get back to her as soon as they heard any news.

Chante was relieved the waiting room was almost empty. She wanted to be alone with her thoughts. She was exhausted from crying. She felt so helpless and so alone.

The door opened and Chante was surprised to see Leo come in. She left him at the café. She glanced at her watch and realized that was hours ago.

"Leo…" Chante cried out haltingly.

Leo saw how totally distraught she was.

"Is he the one, Chante?" Leo asked simply.

Chante realized that word must have gotten around by now. She was with Jared when he got shot. It was in her arms where he collapsed. Talk was rife in a hospital setting and people would make their conclusions whether she liked it or not. The nurses were all probably gossiping about her now and her relationship with Jared Lowell.

Chante remembered how Jared reached for her face and tenderly caressed her cheek before he lost consciousness. The last words he uttered were forever imprinted in her heart.

'I love you, Chante,' she recalled.

Remembering those words triggered a fresh deluge of tears. Her shoulders heaved as she tried to control the surge of her emotions. She was worried sick about him now but Leo needed an answer.

"Yes…," Chante replied.

Leo held her at arm's length and said, "Don't worry…we'll do everything we can to save him."

Then he left.

Chante realized the irony of her situation. She broke up with a man she did not love and now she had to trust that man to save the one she loved.

Chante didn't know how long she sat there before the police came and took her statement. They confirmed what she knew and what the other witnesses saw. Jared pushed her out of harm's way and took the bullet instead.

After they had gone, the door opened once again and Mrs. Samantha Lowell entered the waiting room. She was exactly as Chante remembered her last. Patrician, cool, and collected even if her eyes were red-rimmed with tears.

She approached Chante with arms opened wide. Chante received her embrace and sobbed once again.

"It's all my fault…it should have been me…,"she cried with muffled sobs.

"Then you don't know Jared the way I do. He will protect anyone he loves even if it means putting his own life in danger." Samantha Lowell said.

They both sat down, arms entwined around each other. Somehow Mrs. Lowell knew. Chante didn't know if Jared told her anything about them. Most probably not. But Mrs. Lowell didn't seem the type of woman who would be the last to know.

The room filled up with visitors as the hours ticked by. Chante recognized some of the ranking members of the hospital board. Lawyers, bankers, political luminaries, and well-known media personalities came and made a beeline for Samantha Lowell. Chante marveled at the dignity in which Mrs. Lowell graciously accepted their concern.

Refreshments were brought in, people milled around in small groups, and despite the somber mood, Chante was glad Mrs. Lowell had her friends about.

She tried to make herself as inconspicuous as possible and was glad when Nurse Betty entered the room with some of the other nurses. She looked straight at Chante and shook her head, indicating there was no word yet about Jared's condition.

Chante wondered if she should stay or go. She wasn't family and she didn't want Samantha Lowell's friends to start wondering who she was and why she was here at all. But she was spared the indecision when the door opened and Dr. Leo Cadman entered the room. All eyes turned to him as he approached Mrs. Lowell. You could hear a pin drop with the silence that ensued.

Chante suppressed the urge to run to him for news. That wasn't her place. But she was filled with apprehension and moved forward as the rest of the people did. Leo searched for her face among the crowd that milled around him, saw her, smiled, and then addressed Mrs. Lowell.

"Mr. Lowell will be fine…," Leo announced as a small cheer erupted inside the room.

"We extracted the bullet that was lodged in his shoulder. The other bullet was a bit tricky as it fragmented near his upper right parietal pleura. We had to make sure all the fragments were removed." Leo announced.

"How… how… is he? Is he still sedated?" Mrs. Lowell asked.

Her scratchy voice was the only indication of the strain she must have been carrying since she found out about the shooting.

"Well…" Leo continued scratching his head, perplexed, and aggravated, "he's awake now. I wanted to give him a sedative to allow him to rest and recover. But he was adamant and refused. He said he was feeling fine."

"Oh thank God," Chante mumbled, staggering backward in relief.

Leo looked at Mrs. Lowell sheepishly and continued, "He's asking for…well…he's asking for…"

Leo glanced at Chante before turning back to Mrs. Lowell, "He's asking for you, ma'am."

"Bull crap...," Mrs. Lowell uttered as a few of the guests chuckled. "You don't have to spare this old lady's feelings. I know my son. As much as he would be happy to see me, he'd be happier now to see the woman he loves. He's asking for Chante Green, right?"

"Right…," Leo agreed without hesitation.

Chante heard her name echoed repeatedly across the room. Nurse Betty hugged her as another triumphant cheer erupted from the nurses around the room.

Samantha Lowell drew near and hugged her tightly before declaring for everyone to hear, "Go to him, Chante. Nurse that beautiful man of ours back to health."

And that was all the encouragement Chante needed. She approached Leo and embraced him before whispering a soft 'thank you' in his ear.

Then she walked towards the door as applause followed her every stride. And when she was outside in the hallway, she ran as fast as her feet could carry her. She felt light as a feather; her ankles sprouted unseen wings that carried her swiftly towards the man who held the promise of a glorious future in his hands.

-The End-

If you enjoyed this series, I would appreciate your leaving a review of the book. Good reviews encourage an author to write as well as help books to sell. Good reviews can be just a few short sentences describing what you liked about the book without having a spoiler. If you could spend 30 seconds writing a review, I would appreciate it: you can review this title right now at your favorite retailer.

Here is a preview of **another story** you may enjoy:

I WANT to know who the hell is responsible for this mess!" boomed Hendrick from the front of the boardroom.

Silence filled the room as all the top people in the company stared at Hendrick in awe. They knew he wasn't the kind of guy to be messed with. Considering the company had just been charged with federal and criminal charges for dumping industrial waste into the Arctic Ocean, they knew it was best to stay silent.

"I return from vacation to find the prosecutor in my office to tell me that a company that I built from the ground up to help humanity is being accused of filling the ocean with waste! Waste??" He screamed across the table, his face turning an angry red. Hendrick stopped for a moment to compose himself and looked at each person at the table, assessing their worth.

"Pray it was not one of you frontrunners that made the decision to handle the waste of the company in this manner. Now go, and I expect reports hourly about how we are making this right and where waste should be going from now on."

Everyone got up from the table quickly and filtered out of the room. Hendrick watched them all leave and turned to his right-hand man, Geoffrey, the CEO of the company.

"Tell me you didn't know."

A broad-shouldered man, Geoffrey held an imposing frame that fit well with the red beard that made him appear like a Viking. He was incredibly loyal and a great asset to the company.

"You have known me your whole life Hendrick, I'm sure you know I had nothing to do with dumping waste into the ocean. The person in charge of a decision like that is one of your minions."

"How is it that the owner and CEO of a company had no idea that his own company has been poisoning the ocean?"

"Someone down the line obviously felt it would save the company a lot of money."

Hendrick snorted, "Ya and no one would ever find out that the Arctic Ocean was suddenly polluted? My god they have vessel numbers and everything, it was our guys to be sure, so how do I not know about it?"

"The prosecutors are doing their investigation and so are we. I can guarantee that we will find out who is responsible before anyone else does."

"I'm being prosecuted, Geoffrey! They think I knew about this madness."

"Look you didn't know and they can't prove that you did. You will have your day in court and they will simply have to let it go. They can't pull evidence from thin air so you're safe."

Hendrick went to the side table by the grand picture window. He poured them both a glass of bourbon, handing one to Geoffrey.

"I built this company because I believed in a vision and now our reputation is being smeared. All the while I'm off doing fundraisers and charity events while some asshole is destroying the ocean under my name."

If you enjoyed this sample then look for **Suspicion: Elusive Billionaire Romance Series, Book 1**.

Here is a preview of **another story** you may enjoy:

**Love Disrupted - Ardent Billionaire Romance
Series, Book 1**

DEIRDRE CLARKE stepped out of her apartment
into the hot Los Angeles sun; dusk had fallen, but the
temperature still sat near 100 degrees. Deirdre was
already running late for her gig, so the sight of her ex-
boyfriend Carl standing by her car irritated her even
more than usual. She stomped down the single flight of
stairs and greeted him with hostility.

"I'm late. What the hell do you want?" Deirdre
demanded.

"Can't a man just stop by to see his best girl?" Carl
smiled. His green eyes complimented his mocha skin
and for a moment Deirdre forgot why she'd put up with
his shit for so long. Then she remembered why she'd
stopped.

"I guess you'd better go see her then," she said
roughly. "And let me be on my way."

"Dee… you know I'm talking about you."

"I'm not your girl no more," she answered, "and
I've got somewhere to be."

"Don't be mad, Dee I just came here to check on
you… you alright? What about D'Angelo? You two
need anything? You got rent covered?"

Deirdre's blood boiled and she met his eyes with a
defiant stare. "I don't need a damn thing from you.
D'Angelo and I are not your business anymore."
Deirdre had been responsible for her younger brother
since their mother had gone to prison. D'Angelo was

one of the reasons she'd known she had to get away
from Carl in the first place. The last thing she wanted
was for her brother to see her thug ex-boyfriend as a
role model.

"When are you going to understand that you can't
buy your way back here?" She glared at him.

"Deirdre, we were together almost our whole lives. I
love you. But I'm not trying to buy my way back. I have
a business proposition for you."

"I don't need a job, I have two," she snapped, trying
to open her car door. Carl blocked her way.

"Its easy money Dee… you wouldn't even know it
was here."

"Ah, I see. You think I'll hide drugs or hot shit for
you, after all of the hell you put me through? You think
I'd take that risk for you and your 'boys'?" She snorted
back at him.

"It's just herb, Dee… it's practically legal. And I
don't know why you're so pissed at me. Nothing that
went down was my FAULT!"

"Our windows were SHOT OUT, Carl. You can
stand there all you want and claim it was a random
drive-by, swear it wasn't personal, but I'm not a moron!
You think I didn't know you'd fallen in with Derrick
and his thugs? You think I believed your lies about
where all the money was coming from? I KNEW what
you were doing, and you just denied, denied, denied.
Until our home was shot up... with my brother inside.
Take your shit and get out of my face." Deirdre shoved

him out of the way of her car and escaped inside. She checked her face in the rearview mirror, and then prayed she'd have time to fix her make-up before she had to go onstage.

She stood on stage, in her element. As Lou played along on the black grand piano, Deirdre let all of her emotions flow out to the music. The small crowd gave her their undivided attention as she belted out Trouble, Stormy Weather, and Summertime. Her white, full length gown stood in stark contrast to the milk-chocolate color of her skin.

Deirdre couldn't remember a time when she didn't love to sing. When she was still a young girl, before her father left, her family went to church every Sunday. She loved listening to the soloists in the choir and dreamed of one day standing next to them. But they'd stopped going to church once her father was gone. When D'Angelo was born, Deirdre had tried to get her mother to go back, but she'd refused; D'Angelo's father was against the idea. But soon, he was gone too. Looking back, Deirdre was sure that was when her mother started using drugs, though she didn't realize what was happening at the time. Three years ago, right after Deirdre graduated from high-school, Pauline Clarke had been busted and sentenced to twenty years in a federal prison. Deirdre became D'Angelo's legal guardian, though in all honesty she'd raised him since he was born.

D'Angelo was a good kid, especially considering everything he'd been through. And he was the reason Deirdre hadn't fallen into the same kind of traps the other girls in her neighborhood had found themselves in. She hadn't had any kids, she hadn't gotten messed up on drugs, and she didn't take her clothes off for money. Instead, Deirdre worked as a hotel maid and took college courses online. She'd have loved to go to school on an actual campus, but she couldn't afford childcare for D'Angelo and she refused to turn him into a latchkey kid at eight years old. Deirdre worked while he was at school, and then after dinner they did their homework together.

Thursday nights were different. Those nights were all for Deirdre. She had a standing gig at Fuseli's, an upscale jazz club in the Hollywood foothills. The gig paid just enough for Deirdre to afford her stage-clothes, but she didn't do it for the money.

When she finished her last set, Deirdre took a seat at the bar and ordered herself a beer and a sandwich. As the bartender walked towards the tap, a tall, broad stranger signaled his attention. When he returned to Deirdre, he carried a martini with her draft.

"Dee, a kind gentleman asked me to bring you this and wondered if you'd mind some company?"

Deirdre looked up at Steve and sighed. After her encounter with Carl, she was in no mood to put up with anyone's advances. "Tell him thank you, but I can't possibly accept."

"I don't know… this one's pretty hot, Dee… he's the one down there, in the suit."

"Really Steve, I'm not up for it right now."

"Alright, fine…" he answered in a disapproving, sing-song voice.

Deirdre thought the issue was dealt with as she watched Steve approach the end of the bar to deliver the message. The gorgeous blonde man took the martini, rose, and headed Deirdre's way.

"I'm sorry," she began as he approached, frustrated that he wouldn't take a hint.

"No, I'm sorry." He smiled. "Your friend told me you've had a bad day. You sang beautifully… I sent this as a token of my appreciation, nothing more," he explained, raising the drink. "Why don't you enjoy it? It might make you feel better. Or I could buy you something else, if you'd prefer? Right before I return to my seat, of course."

If you enjoyed this sample then look for **Love Disrupted - Ardent Billionaire Romance Series, Book 1**.

Here is a preview of **another story** you may enjoy:

Love Anew - Lonely Billionaire Romance Series, Book 1

TRICIA REACHED for another blanket. "Are you cold?" she asked.

Rebecca's breath was raspy as she responded. As her lungs shut down due to ALS, or Amyotrophic Lateral Sclerosis, her ability to speak had started to decline. Muscle by muscle, ALS targeted the body and made it impossible for the individual to live a normal life. It had started a few years ago with Rebecca's legs. Now, her lung muscles were starting to freeze as well. Tricia winced as she thought about the future. If Rebecca chose to use machines to stay alive, her entire body would eventually stop working. At some point, her mind would remain functioning and she would be locked into her body.

Rebecca managed to squeeze out a feeble yes. Reaching over to the cupboard, Tricia removed a blanket and carefully tucked her in. Tricia had spent years training to be a nurse and really liked her job. Since she was an excellent nurse, she had caught the eye of the billionaire, John, at one of the couple's many trips to hospitals around the country. He had noticed the love and care she took with each patient. After a moment's hesitation, Tricia had allowed him to convince her to take care of his wife.

Pictures of Rebecca dotted the room. Since she was unable to leave, John had striven to make her room look like favorite memories of her life and activities. A young, healthy Rebecca smiled in each photo. In the few years she had been physically active, she had acquired awards for horseback riding, cooking and other projects. Now, though, this time of physical fitness had passed. Instead of dashing through the fields on her favorite horse, Rebecca spent her time in this room. She had taken her difficulties in stride and was truly brave in the face of all of these medical issues.

Finishing with the blanket, Rebecca started to say something. Leaning closer to hear her, Tricia finally pulled up a chair. "What do you need, Rebecca?" she queried.

Sighing, Rebecca whispered, "I need to talk to John. I have to tell him how I want to die."

Squeezing her hand, Tricia nodded. "Once I leave your room, I will go get him. Just in case he is not around, did you want me to give him a message?"

Rebecca tried to nod, but her head did not respond all the way. "Yes, I do. You need to tell him that I do not want any machines. He could keep me alive forever with a breathing tube, but I do not want to live a life where I am permanently locked into my body. And," she paused and struggled to take another breath. "I do not want him to stop enjoying life or waiting around for my eventual death. If God wants to take my soul now, we should not interfere."

Tricia nodded sadly. Most patients with ALS were more afraid of being stuck within their minds than actual death. She understood, but she could not imagine what life would be like without Rebecca's gentle soul. "I will tell him," she said.

Leaving the room, Tricia traversed the hallways of the mansion. John had built his fortune by buying and selling real estate properties. His initial money had arrived through an early investment in the dot com boom before the bubble burst. After seeing the dangers of the stock market, he had started to just buy and rent out properties. Even with the recent recession, he still made a profit. Instead of selling his properties or developing, he had continued to rent them out. In a decade or two, he had talked of selling and retiring. His plans had arrived before his wife had been diagnosed with ALS. Unwilling to speak of his life after her future death, Tricia had not asked about any change in his future plans.

The halls of the house were dotted with white oak doorways that led to a myriad of rooms. Plush white carpet softly surrounded Tricia's feet as she walked. She dreaded the conversation that was about to happen. Every day, she updated John about the status of his wife. Unfortunately, she seldom had good news to share. She nodded to John's secretary as she entered the office. Unlike most rich men, he used a male secretary. Before talking had become so difficult, Rebecca had explained that he tried to hire primarily males so that Rebecca would never worry about his fidelity. Since Tricia was intended to cater just to his wife, she had been allowed to work there despite her gender.

If you enjoyed this sample then look for **Love Anew - Lonely Billionaire Romance Series, Book 1**.

Other Books by Shyla Starr

- Persuasive Billionaire BWWM Romance Series

- Tenacious Billionaire BWWM Romance Series

- Elusive Billionaire Romance Series

- Lonely Billionaire Romance Series

- Ardent Billionaire Romance Series

- Fervent Billionaire BWWM Romance Series

Get the latest update on new releases from the author at:

https://shylastarr.com/newsletter/

About the Author - Shyla Starr

Shyla currently specializes in writing interracial romance stories and is a huge fan of the alpha male. Simply put, there just aren't enough stories about mixed couple romances, which is something she is aiming to fix.

Being a bookworm all her life, when Shyla discovered men she also realized how easy it was to fulfill her fantasies through her writing.

When not writing and fantasizing about men, Shyla enjoys dancing, reading and chilling with her friends.

Connect with Shyla Starr

I really appreciate you reading my book! Here are my social media coordinates:

Friend me on Facebook: https://www.facebook.com/shylastarrauthor

Follow me on Twitter: https://twitter.com/shylstarr

Check me out on Goodreads: https://www.goodreads.com/author/show/8436084.Shyla_Starr

Subscribe to my newsletter: https://shylastarr.com/newsletter/

Visit my website: https://shylastarr.com/